MW01118359

ABOUT THIS BOOK

Welcome to Havenwood Falls, a small town in the majestic mountains of Colorado. A town where legacies began centuries ago, bloodlines run deep, and dark secrets abound. A town where nobody is what you think, where truths pose as lies, and where myths blend with reality. A place where everyone has a story. Including the high schoolers. This is only but one . . .

Like all young witch hunters in Havenwood Falls, seventeen-year-old Macy Blackstone has been spelled to control her killer instincts. When she's reawakened too early, though, her world flips upside down.

Daughter to the Blackstone witch hunters' matriarch, Macy should have known what was coming, but her mother hadn't prepared her. Overwhelmed with the surge of energy from the new moon coupled with a solar eclipse, she's unable to handle the new sensations, and she flees town. To her surprise, she discovers an entire family branch of witch hunters living nearby. Only, the more she gets to know them, the more she learns about their dark intentions for both the witches and the Blackstones of Havenwood Falls.

Gallad Augustine, witch and boyfriend extraordinaire, possesses powerful magic, but Macy took off too soon for him to help her. Now, as her soul mate, his connection to her heart may be the only way for anyone to reach her.

Macy has one moon cycle—twenty-eight days—to uncover the witch hunters' plans and return home before the town's wards wipe her memory permanently and she forgets everything about her family, her home, and her one true love. And if she can't remember them, she won't be able to save them.

REAWAKENED

A HAVENWOOD FALLS HIGH NOVELLA

MORGAN WYLIE

HAVENWOOD FALLS HIGH BOOKS

Written in the Stars by Kallie Ross
Reawakened by Morgan Wylie
The Fall by Kristen Yard
Somewhere Within by Amy Hale
Awaken the Soul by Michele G. Miller

More books releasing on a monthly basis

Stay up to date at www.HavenwoodFalls.com

OTHER BOOKS BY MORGAN WYLIE

❦

YA FANTASY

Silent Orchids (Book 1)

Veiled Shadows (Book 2)

Daegan (Novella 2.5)

Fractured Darkness (Book 3)

Fading Light (Book 4) (Fall 2017)

The Sol-lumieth (Book 5) (Winter 2017)

The Rise of the Paladin (An Alandria Short Story Prequel) (Free with Newsletter subscription)

❦

YA PARANORMAL/SUPERNATURAL

HAILEY: The Necromancer (A Shadow Realm Novella 1) (previously released as Supernatural Chronicles: The Necromancers Novella #7)

JAX: The Doppelgänger (A Shadow Realm Novella 2)

WILLOW (A Shadow Realm Novella 3) (Coming soon!)

SOLANGE (A Shadow Realm Novella 4) (Coming soon!)

❦

NA/ADULT PARANORMAL ROMANCE

RYLEN (The Tangled Web Book 1)
MATHER (The Tangled Web Book 2)
JET (A Tangled Web Novella) (Exclusive in the Creatures Box Set)

COLLECTIONS

Supernatural Chronicles: New Orleans Collection
(The Necromancers: Novella #7)

Copyright © 2017 Morgan Wylie, Ang'dora Productions, LLC

All rights reserved.

Published by

Ang'dora Productions, LLC

5621 Strand Blvd, Ste 210

Naples, FL 34110

Havenwood Falls and Ang'dora Productions and their associated logos are trademarks and/or registered trademarks of Ang'dora Productions, LLC.

Cover design by Regina Wamba at MaeIDesign.com

Except as permitted under the U.S. Copyright Act of 1976, no part of this publication may be reproduced, stored in a retrieval system, or transmitted in any form or by any means, electronic, mechanical, photocopying, recording, or otherwise, without written permission of the owner of this book.

Please do not participate in or encourage piracy of copyrighted materials in violation of the author's rights. Purchase only authorized editions.

This book is a work of fiction. Names, characters and events are either products of the author's imagination or are used fictitiously, and any resemblance to actual persons, living or dead, is entirely coincidental.

Ebook ISBN: 978-1-939859-41-9

Print ISBN: 978-1-939859-42-6

This story is dedicated to YOU, the reader. I hope you have as much fun in Havenwood Falls as I have had!

I can't wait for you to meet the Blackstone family!

CHAPTER 1

ost seventeen-year-olds about to enter their senior year of high school enjoyed every last bit of their summer break. Some even went on vacations. Not me—Macy Blackstone, witch hunter. All I wanted to do was forget the title and be normal at least for a day, but apparently that day was not today.

Nearing the end of August in Havenwood Falls, Colorado, the weather had already began to change—not that it ever stayed any particular temperature for long. Up in the mountains especially, fall came earlier than in the lower elevations. The nights grew chilly earlier, and mornings like this one reminded me what I loved about fall.

Cozy in my oversized, chunky cable-knit wrap sweater, I snuggled into the corner of a large outdoor sectional sofa in front of a giant rock fireplace. Stretching out my legging-clad legs, complete with warm Uggs on my feet, I sighed with contentment. I watched the town come to life below me while I slowly sipped from the steaming mug of coffee in my hand. Rays from the sunrise streaked down to touch the edge of our deck, stretching as far as the fire pit and the uncovered section of deck. The reverse would happen just the same again at sunset. Tipping my head up, I closed my eyes, absorbing warmth from the sun's kiss as it crept up my face, inching as far as the roof above would allow it.

"Beautiful, isn't it?" My mom's voice floated from the doorway separating the kitchen from the outside living area.

"It is," I answered, looking back at her. My mom, Lilith Blackstone, was a beautiful woman, appearing in her mid-forties—though she was actually a bit older. For a human, she looked forty-five, but as a hunter, she was still relatively young at seventy-eight years old. Most of the women in my family were hunters—witch hunters to be exact, though we didn't actively hunt witches. My mom was descended from the founding Blackstone family, a strong lineage of witch hunters. She also held a seat on the Court of the Sun and the Moon as the representative and matriarch for our entire family.

"Are you seeing Gallad today?" she asked, moving toward the railing, carrying her own steaming mug.

"I'm supposed to meet him at the vineyard pretty soon, actually." I checked the time on my phone.

Her eyes were on me, watching me, the weight of her assessing stare boring into me. Turning to face her, I couldn't place her expression. Was she upset? She seemed more questioning than anything else.

"Is something wrong, Mom?"

"How are you feeling?" she returned, avoiding my question.

"Um, fine thanks, but don't think I am that easily diverted. What's up?"

Coming over to me, she placed her hand on the back of my neck, now free from my silky blonde locks since I piled them on top of my head in a messy bun that morning. "How is your injury?"

"It's much better since the witches gave us that healing salve to put on it." Reflexively, I touched the back of my neck as well after she pulled away. "There's some scabbing where the stupid tree limb tore my flesh off, but otherwise I think it's good. See?" I pulled the neck of my sweater down, and tugged my T-shirt back for her to see it.

In a reckless attempt to be normal, I had climbed a tree and tried to jump to an adjacent tree like some damn spider-monkey wannabe. The new tree didn't want to be my friend and wouldn't let me grab hold of it until I had slid down part way, taking my flesh off as I went.

"Your hunter marking looks to be untouched. However, your protection tattoo got a bit roughed up. Did you have Saundra Beaumont look at it like I asked?"

Saundra Beaumont sat on the high council of the Luna Coven, making her one of the most powerful witches in town.

Since I was born, my parents and the Court knew what I would become based on a stupid skin discoloration on the back of my neck in the shape of a cluster of small stars. All hunters were born with it, like a birthmark—or a beacon of doom.

"Yes, Mom. She said it looked fine, and I shouldn't have any issues with the wards within my tattoo. Addie looked at it, too. She said she'd need to touch up a few of the lines but would wait until the skin was fully healed. They both agreed the tattoo held enough magic that it shouldn't be an issue to wait until it was time for the permanent one."

In Havenwood Falls, all the supernatural residents received a tattoo infused with magic. The markings were there for not only our protection, but also for the town's. They protected each individual race, but also helped temper and conceal magic from our human residents, who made up about half of our population. Visitors also had to register with the Court of the Sun and Moon to receive a temporary tattoo for the duration of their stay.

As I grew older, into double digits, the Luna Coven placed a magical, invisible-to-the-eye marking in the shape of a crescent moon with a dragon right below my birthmark. The tattoo was a temporary marking intended to suppress any hunter tendencies until I turned eighteen. According to our traditions as witch hunters, at the age of eighteen we go through a ceremony, committing ourselves to abide by the rules and laws of Havenwood Falls. Hunters can choose for themselves then if they are going to go out on their own, never to return to Havenwood Falls, or become a suppressed member of the Blackstone family and town at large. Good options, right? Normal human high schoolers didn't have to deal with that kind of crap. Choice made and ritual completed, we then receive the permanent tattoo of an adult, thus becoming an official citizen of Havenwood Falls.

"Speaking of which, Macy, I need to speak with you about your upcoming birthday and marking ceremony." A slight edge laced Mom's words, anticipating my reply.

I sighed. This was an old conversation. My eighteenth birthday was coming up the beginning of October.

"Mom, we've talked about this. I still have some time. Can we not talk about it yet? School is starting soon and I want to enjoy the last of summer. Since I can't go anywhere interesting, I want to try to be as normal as possible while I still can." Even I could hear the bitterness and whiny petulance in my tone.

"Macy," she practically growled enough to rival one of the Kasun wolves. The Kasuns were not only the largest werewolf pack in Havenwood Falls, but their alpha, Ric Kasun, was also the town sheriff. "You have put this off for too long. The ceremony will happen, and you need to be prepared. There are things you should know and things to prepare for."

Jumping up from my no-longer-quiet space, I faced her. Then she did something I was not expecting. Moving to the side, she revealed another woman standing behind her in the kitchen, watching the interaction with a frown. Looking from the new arrival back to my mother, I scowled.

"You brought Grandma into this?" Fury pulsed through my veins. I loved my grandmother, and I was normally a reasonable—okay, *somewhat* reasonable—person, but she went behind my back like I needed some kind of intervention.

Eva Blackstone, aka Grandma, was regularly brought in when my mom didn't get her way—at least it looked that way to us kids, my two brothers and myself.

"Now, Macy, be rational. There are many details to attend to and your orientation to complete," Grandma chided from the kitchen, beckoning me inside. Tall, slender, and confident, my grandmother held an air of regality and pride. Her hair had been a fierce blond bob since I could remember, mirroring the same edge in her personality.

"This is my last year of high school, and I'll spend most of it as an official Blackstone hunter. I just want to spend the rest of my summer as an irresponsible teenager. Is that too much to ask?" I huffed and folded my arms across my chest.

"Yes, it is," Grandma said flatly. "You have a responsibility to this family and this town. It is time you owned up to it."

I put my mug in the sink and took several slow drags of air, cooling my growing temper.

"Macy, nothing changes once you are marked. It's all in your head," Grandma added.

I shot a glance toward my mom still standing in the doorway. Her gaze was off in the distance, watching the rising sun or something else farther away, locked in the recesses of her mind. Distracted, she finally felt my stare and looked back to me. I frowned.

"I don't know about that, Grandma," I whispered. My mom definitely had times when she was off, but lately, it had been more obvious. She was hiding something, but I didn't know what.

"Oh that's ridiculous, child. You have until the end of summer and then you will take your place in this town as a Blackstone hunter or . . ."

I spun my head in her direction, mouth open wide. "There's an 'or' in your sentence?"

"Macy, you know the rules of Havenwood Falls. If a witch hunter will not choose to be permanently marked, they cannot remain a resident here," my mother interjected. "And because of the memory wards around the borders, whoever chooses not to stay and follow the laws will forget everything about Havenwood Falls, including their family."

"I know the laws, but I don't need my family threatening me with them either." My heart suddenly felt heavy and sad. I knew they didn't mean to hurt me, but still they did. I grabbed my messenger bag off the counter and moved swiftly through the large, rustic yet modern kitchen-dining-great room toward the front door.

"Where are you going, young lady?" Grandma's voice echoed through the room.

"I'm meeting Gallad at the vineyard, then I have to go into the square to pick up my check at Broastful Brews." I sighed, then schooled my voice to an acceptable tone. "I'm sorry, I just need some space. I'll be back later."

"Let her go, Mom. I'll talk to her again later." My mom's voice reached me before I opened the front door.

CHAPTER 2

took the shortcut from my house in Havenwood Heights over to Stone Falls Winery without having to head down to the main road. My brothers and I had cut through the fields and forest since we were little, thus wearing down our own path from our main house to our home away from home at the vineyard.

My family had several businesses, including the one I headed to now. Stone Falls Winery had been in my family for generations—since the first hunter, Marie Blackstone, had set up camp. More recently, we added Soothing Sips, a wine-tasting bar in town square, and NamaStays Inn at the Vineyard—a quaint B&B boasting six cabins with picturesque mountain views set amidst the vineyard. My family added them about ten years ago, when we started to see more tourists and visitors to the town.

My father, Reginald "Reggie" Benton Blackstone—the men who married into our family took the Blackstone name—was human and ran the daily operations of the vineyard. Even the extended family was heavily involved with each endeavor, always had been. Grandma's cousin, Great Aunt Letti—Letitia Blackstone, former family matriarch—even oversaw the Yoga in the Vines classes, and she was practically 116 years old! Okay, so she looked like she was in her seventies, but still. Long life ran in the Blackstone family.

Everything about Stone Falls Winery was designed to bring soothing relaxation to your senses, and calm was a necessity for the hunters of my family. The drives and instincts of the witch hunters were strong even with the Luna's magic suppressing the bulk of it. At just the right height, the winery sat above the town providing a view of all of town square. When night blanketed the valley, the town lights and sounds mesmerized even the grumpiest of guests. But when a large moon crested over the tips of the craggy peaks, the sight stopped me in my tracks; I could stare for hours like nothing else mattered. I had memories from when I was small of reaching up, thinking I could touch the tip of the moon because it appeared so close.

Several buildings, modern yet mixed with rustic architecture— similar to our home—were laid out with designed precision. Each was positioned to ensnare the majestic views of snow-capped, jagged mountains.

I maneuvered my way quickly through those buildings, hoping to not get caught by Aunt Letti, lest I be roped into some odd job I was not assigned today. Plus, I already had plans.

"You really shouldn't text and walk at the same time. You're liable to miss something right in front of you." Gallad's voice arrested me. I smiled. Leaning against the back wall of NamaStay's lobby, with one booted foot propped up behind him and sheltered in the shade from the roof line, Gallad was the image of a bad boy in his black leather jacket covering a rock band T-shirt accompanied by gray-washed jeans.

"You really shouldn't wait in the shadows for people. Someone might think you were stalking them." I tried to shake off the small fright with sarcastic wit, but my accelerated heart rate said otherwise. When I looked into his eyes, however, my nerves calmed. His love and concern packaged with his cute signature lopsided grin took my breath away.

"You're right." He pushed off from the wall and moved in close. His cologne wrapped around me, the intoxicating aroma pulling me in close. I loved the way he smelled of pine and spices—it made me feel cozy and safe every time. "I'm sorry. I bet I can make it up to you." His grin turned from innocent to devilish in a matter of seconds as he leaned in to steal a kiss. In that moment, I felt our connection—I was home.

Gallad Augustine, grandson to another Luna Coven High Council member, was a witch prodigy. Remarkably handsome with his windswept dark hair, fair skin, and bright green eyes, he was truly an all-around good guy—though he wore the exterior of a bad boy at times—and he was my boyfriend. Yes, it was unheard of for a witch hunter to date a witch, but stranger things had happened in Havenwood Falls.

I couldn't help but cover my heart with my hand. The beats sped up when he was near—they always did. Those girlish butterflies took flight in my stomach no matter how much I tried to suppress them.

"You definitely have a way of making it up to me," I mumbled in a swoony state. If anyone had told me I would be the type to swoon, I would have laughed in their face. But Gallad could make me swoon pretty much without trying. Grabbing my hand, he laced his fingers in mine and pulled me alongside him as we strolled through the vines of grapes.

"Have you seen any of the Perseids meteor shower? I saw several shooting across the sky last night. It was amazing, Gallad." I couldn't help the awe I heard in my own voice, but they were truly a sight to see.

Gallad's face turned down to me with a smile so big it reached his eyes. "I did. The meteors looked like shooting stars." He looked up as if he could see them already, but the sky still had plenty of color. "I thought of you the whole time, wishing I was lying on the ground somewhere with you, watching the meteors together."

I blushed. The rush of heat ran up my neck and into my face. Squeezing his hand in mine, I changed the subject. "How was your morning?"

He shrugged casually. "Pretty uneventful. You?"

Frowning, I didn't want to talk about my morning. *Way to start a conversation you didn't want to participate in, Macy,* I scolded myself. Too late—he caught my frown.

"What's wrong, Mace?"

"My mom tried to push the marking ceremony on me again." I

sighed. "This time she brought my grandmother in on it. That didn't go over too well."

Running my fingers through the tendrils of hair that slipped down from my messy bun, I felt guilty for bringing the topic up. "I'm sorry. I didn't want to drag you into it."

"What are boyfriends for if not to be there when needed?" His cute smile melted my heart and soothed my guilt.

"Thank you," I said sheepishly.

"Hey, how is your back where you were almost skinned alive by a revenge-hungry tree?"

I laughed out loud. "That tree *was* out for revenge, wasn't it?" Shifting my shoulder blades as if testing out my injury for his benefit, I smiled. "It's almost healed."

Gallad kept quiet as we continued walking, but I felt him glance my way several times. I could practically feel the wheels turning in his head.

"Come out with it already, before you burst."

He blew out a gush of air and raked the fingers of his free hand through the hair sliding down into his eyes. "I know you don't need me to add to it, but you know how important your permanent tattoo is. I'm sure Cousin Addie would do it as soon as your skin fully heals."

"She would, and she offered." Slowly, I brought air in through my nose as I calmed my inner nerves. The idea of being permanently chained left me raw, no matter how much I loved my town. I mean, I knew I'd be able to leave town someday. Since I was little, I always wanted to step outside the boundaries of Havenwood Falls—even just for one day, to see what else was out there, how other people lived, what it might be like to live in a normal town. Just once. I wanted to travel!

Mom and Dad left often for short business meetings and quick getaways, but they had never taken me or my younger brother, Brice. They always returned within the necessary twenty-eight-day moon cycle. In fact, they had never risked more than two weeks. As a human, my older brother Brock got to go with them a couple times, and even had tried attending college outside of town, but he didn't have much desire, it seemed, to travel. I would do anything to leave for college, but apparently it wasn't in my cards—or so I'd been told—because I was marked as a hunter. Literally. Alas, I would have to wait a little while longer. Until then, I would do what I could to pretend I was a normal seventeen-year-old, headed into her senior year at Havenwood Falls High.

"I'm just not ready yet."

"I won't push you, Mace. But I have plans for us, you and me, and don't want anything to get in the way of them." Gallad turned a smile on me that rivaled a rogue pirate.

My heart thumped up into my throat. All salivary glands stopped working at once, drying out my mouth. And those damn butterflies took flight so fast, they almost knocked me off my feet. Words. I couldn't find words.

Gallad laughed at me. He actually laughed. "It's all right, Macy. Seems I caught you off guard." Turning toward me, he grabbed my other hand and tugged me close, so close I could feel his chest rise and fall with each breath.

"Ha! Just a bit," I forced out shakily.

Gallad let go of one of my hands. He brought his up and tucked a stray hair behind my ear. His fingers skimmed lightly over my face, sending shockwaves of excitement through my body and launching those same butterflies into a frenzy. Just when I thought he was going to kiss me, his forehead rested against mine. His voice lowered, and he said, "I love you, Macy. And I think about the future with you. There's no question in my mind we were meant to be together."

"You're my other half, Gallad. My soul mate," I whispered in return. For some reason, I couldn't say the "L" word just yet, though I felt it about to bubble over the rim of my heart.

We stayed forehead to forehead, standing in a row of grape vines for more than a couple minutes. At least until we heard some of the workers headed into that section of the vines. Gallad pulled back just enough to get a better angle, then came in for a gentle, teasing kiss; long enough for me to feel cherished but short enough to make me want him more.

Hand in hand, we walked out of the vines and headed for the road to take us into town.

"You headed to work?" I asked him.

"Yep. Where you off to next?"

"I don't work today, but I need to grab my paycheck, and I'll meet Ruby in the square for lunch."

Once we walked out from the main entrance of Stone Falls Winery, we hit Blackstone Road. Just sayin'—it's pretty cool to have a road named after your family. Casually, we chatted as we walked together, slowing down as we approached the intersection at Eighth.

"I'll call you later. Have fun with Ruby," he said as he left me with a peck on the cheek.

"Bye, Gallad."

I watched him walk away toward the Sun and Moon Academy. During the summer, Gallad worked in the private school's *Histories for Supernaturals* program, a course for those who wanted to learn more about their heritage—humans not included. The Luna Coven had made available most of the information they had collected on all the races for the program. Gallad hoped to one day be positioned high up within his own family, the Augustines, and on the Luna Coven's council. In order to do so, it was required he learn the histories of all the supernaturals in town. He gave off the vibes of a bad boy, but deep down he was actually quite the bookworm. The Luna Coven basically ran the town—you didn't want to cross them or the rules of Havenwood Falls—but they also protected us from the outside world and from each other.

Gallad turned back and blew me a kiss. Why something so simple could make me blush even from a distance, I would never know, but it warmed my heart. I waved back and headed down Eighth Street toward the town square—the heart of Havenwood Falls.

CHAPTER 3

*R*uby Jean Milton—my best friend—stood waiting for me at the corner of Eighth and Stuart Streets, outside the entrance to Broastful Brew, where I worked as a part-time barista. Her strawberry-blond hair blew into her face as she wrestled it into a ponytail high on her head. I laughed. She hadn't spotted me yet. Ruby, who wasn't human, either, but came from a family of lynx shifters, looked up just as I passed in front of the firehouse. Her warm brown eyes lit up with her smile.

"Ruby!" I waved, crossing the street toward her.

"Hi, Macy! You're late. I bet you just couldn't tear yourself away from Gallad's kisses." Her hands crossed over her heart, and she sighed dramatically.

She could always make me laugh. "Not quite."

"Don't spoil my visions of the two of you, Macy Marie Blackstone. I don't have my own love life right now, so I live vicariously through yours."

"All right, so maybe there was some kissing and hand holding then." I winked at her. Ruby came at me with arms wide open. I let her embrace me, not that I had a choice in the matter. Ruby was a hugger; always had been, ever since we met in kindergarten. She was also the most loyal person I knew—and that said a lot, since I was born in Havenwood Falls and I knew everyone . . . mostly.

"I knew it!" Ruby declared with a fist of victory and a giggle as she pulled away from me.

"I just need a minute to run in and grab my check, then we can go get lunch and more coffee over at Coffee Haven."

"Why don't we just stay here?" Ruby frowned. "I mean, isn't it strange that you go in to one coffee shop to get paid to then spend said money over at a different coffee shop?"

"Well, yeah it sounds strange when you say it that way." I laughed. "I don't want to feel like I'm at work. Plus Broastful Brew is usually filled with the older residents or the morning meeting clientele. I want to feel the energy over at Coffee Haven."

"Then that's what we're going to do." Ruby nodded her head decidedly. "Go get your check. Hurry, though. I'm hungry and I can't wait to see what Willow made today!"

Willow Fairchild was the owner of Coffee Haven and, being one of the fae, a strong empath.

I ducked into Broastful Brew and breathed a lungful of freshly brewed coffee. A low din of chatter filled the atmosphere, but it felt more like a library than a coffee shop. I waved to some of the regulars, but headed toward the employee area. Mabel, the owner of the shop, manned the register. She smiled at me and said hello as soon as she finished with her customer.

"Morning, Mabel, I'm just grabbing my check."

"Morning to you, too, Macy. It's in the usual place on the desk in the office, dear. Would you like a coffee to go?"

"No, thank you, I had one at home this morning already."

As quick as I could, I retrieved my check and snuck back out while Mabel visited with a customer. Otherwise I'd be leaving with another coffee.

On our way to Coffee Haven, we passed Backwoods Sport & Ski and Howe's Herbal Shoppe, owned by Ruby Howe but now run by her daughter, Rose.

"Hello, Ms. Howe." I waved to the older woman as she swept her walkway, muttering under breath. She barely raised her head to look at us, let alone wave back. Ruby and I exchanged a smile—the old woman added her own flavor to the morning.

We found a table outside at Coffee Haven, then placed our order. Coffee Haven was quite the popular place even at lunchtime; the interior was abuzz with voices and activity. For some reason, the white noise satisfied something internally with me, but it was such a nice day, so we stayed outside.

Sighing, I slumped and took my seat. Ruby took hers across from me. I shifted in my seat, pulled at the neck of my sweater, and ultimately took the thing off; it was warm now that the sun was high in the blue August sky.

"Does it hurt?" Ruby asked, watching me intently.

"No, it itches. I think it's irritated or something. I either need more salve or to get it checked again." Not realizing I did it, I reached over my shoulder and attempted to scratch where the itching was most intense.

Ruby's frown intensified. "I'd get it checked."

Her head shot up and looked at something behind me. "Gallad's mom approaching," she whispered under her hand suddenly in front of her mouth.

Whipping my head around, I spotted her myself.

"Covert, Macy." Ruby's sarcasm complemented her eye roll.

"Subtlety is not one of my qualities, you should know that."

"Good afternoon, ladies," Mrs. Augustine greeted as she approached our table.

"Hello, Mrs. Augustine," we said in unison, and sounded like schoolgirl robots.

"How are you?" I added quickly after.

"Fine, dear, but please, I've told you, call me Ronya," Gallad's mom corrected. Ronya's bright smile was so much like her son's; it was like an explosion of joy and good looks all at once. Gliding in, wearing leggings and a flowing chiffon tunic, she turned her joyous expression, accompanied by her long and curly dark hair, toward me. "Good to see you, Macy. You, too, Ruby, dear."

"You, too, Ronya," I replied with not as much gusto as I would have

15

normally, but something felt . . . off. Again? What was going on? Absently, I scratched my bare arms. The itch persisted, and I wanted nothing more than to scratch my skin off. I sat on my hands before my nails drew blood.

Ronya's sharp and intense eyes evaluated me. "Macy? Are you feeling all right?"

"Yes, I'm fine. The scrape on my back is itching its way to a complete healing."

Ronya's gaze traveled to my neck and shoulder then back to my eyes as a new frown formed. "Maybe you should get it checked again. Injuries have a tendency to get worse if left untreated."

An unexpected sensation suddenly rose in me—like something inside me clawed to get out, something agitated . . . something dark.

"Thank you. I had Ms. Beaumont look at it already. You know how scabs itch when they heal." My laugh sounded hollow even to me. "I'll get her to look at it again."

"See that you do, dear." Ronya's pointed stare pinned me in my seat and made me feel small. Fear uncharacteristically reared its ugly face in her eyes. "A darkness stirs inside you. I can see it, and I fear for you— and my son." She spoke quietly so no one next to us would hear, then turned and walked away.

Rage boiled in my chest. Like I would ever hurt Gallad! He was my other half. My soul recognized him like no other.

"Whoa! She did not just say that!" Ruby gasped. Her hand found mine on the table and gave it a squeeze. "Mace, you okay? Don't worry about her. She must be having an off day."

"Or I am." Unexpectedly, I was afraid for the first time that I really didn't know what would happen to me if I wasn't protected by my Havenwood Falls tattoo. "What if the magic in my marking didn't hold up from the injury?"

Would I really not be able to control the hunter within me? Was that what this was all about?

"Don't be so dramatic. I'm sure you're fine," Ruby encouraged, but her tone lacked the usual confidence. Ruby leaned forward and whispered, "Saundra Beaumont, the head of the Luna Coven herself, checked it. If she says the magic is intact, then it is."

Slowly, the blood drained away from my face until it became lead in my feet. "What if she was wrong?"

"Nope, I don't buy it." Ruby looked around at nearby tables at Coffee Haven. Many of the lunchtime crowd had moved on or gone back to work. Only a few stragglers like ourselves enjoyed the last rays of the season. "You look like you've seen a ghost."

"Hmm?" Shifting my back against the chair, itching what I couldn't reach with my hand, I finally noticed Ruby staring at me. Concern and alarm briefly flashed across her eyes before it flitted away. "Don't look at me like that, Ruby Jean Milton. I'll be fine, you'll see. They'll all see."

Ruby laughed. She could have been hurt or put off by me, but instead she pushed back. "There you are. Come on back to the now."

"You're right. Sorry."

"Before I get going, remember tomorrow is the eclipse?" Her eyes lit up with excitement.

"You know we don't get a total eclipse here, right?" I hated to burst her bubble but I didn't think it was going to be as spectacular as she imagined it would be.

"Of course I do. I've learned all about it. I got us glasses, too!"

I didn't like the sound of silly party glasses. Wrinkling up my nose I asked her, "What for?"

"To protect our eyes, silly."

"Of course." Rolling my eyes, I flopped back in my chair. "Tell me again why this is a memorable moment?"

Ruby sighed, but of course I knew she wanted to tell me more about it. "So this is special for several reasons. This particular solar eclipse happened like thirty-eight years ago but it also falls on a new moon. But not only that—"

"Interesting," I slipped in.

"No, listen, Mace! This *is* interesting." Leaning forward, she slapped my thigh, gaining my attention. "This new moon is a Black Moon, ushering in a total solar eclipse. This is a rare combination of events that especially witches love because of the heightened power unleashed."

Sitting forward, I absorbed all she said. "That actually is interesting. I feel like I've heard some of it before." I pinched the bridge of my nose, racking my brain. "Oh! I remember Gallad told me the witches planned a ritual to strengthen the magical protection wards around the schools after the Parade of the Perseids tomorrow night. Apparently, the darkness from the new moon would be the best time for it."

"That makes sense. It's also during the meteor showers—there should be increased supernatural energy streaking above us—not a bad plan." Ruby nodded her approval. She didn't have a single magic bone in her body, but she loved to know all the things going on she could—a bit of a busybody if you asked me, but that was one of the things I loved about her. One of the other things I loved about her was her ability to quickly shift subject matters.

"Speaking of the parade, are you coming by after work tomorrow to see the finished product?" Her face stretched tight in nervous anticipation.

I laughed out loud, startling a nearby coffee drinker. "You look like a lizard."

"I'm worried our float won't be good enough," she admitted.

"I saw what those wolves were working on, and the Kasuns' float looks pretty good, but I think ours is up there, too—it maybe even has a chance at winning." Folding my arms across my chest, I held tight so as not to scratch. "I'm not sure the Luna Coven will be able to pull it off this year. Pretty sure the trophy will have a new mantel to sit on," I rambled. I rarely ever rambled unless I was nervous or trying to keep my mind off something else, which apparently I was doing.

Ruby huffed. "Oh gods, you're like a prepubescent shifter before their first full moon. Can you not hold still? It's like you're reacting to the pull of the moon or something."

I inhaled sharply. "Well, that's ridiculous. I'm not a shifter." If I kept furrowing my brow, I was going to get a headache. "Why would I be reacting to the moon? I never have had a reaction before. Oh, maybe I *am* a shifter!"

So maybe I was being a little dramatic, but my skin crawled, begging me to scratch it.

"All right. You're losing it. That's my cue to leave."

"Take me or leave me! You'll feel bad when I shift, and you aren't there to guide me through it." Shrugging my shoulders, I gave her a wink.

"I'll keep ya! Where you headed now?"

"I'm supposed to stop in at Soothing Sips. Brock's there and will drive me home since he's coming for dinner." My older brother Brock had moved into his own gorgeous cabin-esque townhouse in Havenstone.

"Bye."

Hugging Ruby, I squeezed extra tight, and she returned the love. Her information about the new moon and the eclipse triggered a thought in my mind—or gut—that I wanted to follow up on tonight with my computer.

CHAPTER 4

*S*oothing Sips, my family's wine-tasting bar on the east side of the square, served as a front to the more nefarious side to the Blackstone's endeavors for Havenwood Falls.

I headed north through the center of town square toward the fountain. Beautiful and sparkling at the interior, the fountain was gifted by Mayor Barbie Stuart's ancestors when the town was founded. Town square was a popular hangout, especially when the weather was nice. Several people simply loitered, basking in the sun, while others used the opportunity to exercise around the square. Spotting Viv Freeman and her best friend Zara Shannon jogging, I waved to them. Both waved back excitedly. They were also seniors at school, and I hoped we would be in classes together this year again.

I was about to cross the street to Soothing Sips when tendrils of unease crawled down my spine, and I broke out in a cold sweat. A toxicity rose in my stomach, bile forcing its way up my throat. Running —faster than normally possible for me—to the closest garbage bin, I expelled all the wonderful lunch I had just eaten.

"Oh no," I moaned. I gripped the garbage can as dizziness threatened to steal the ground out from under my feet. Swaying, I held on tight.

20

"Macy?" My brother's voice broke through the haze fogging my brain. He jogged toward me, concern written all over his face.

"Macy? Are you all right? I called you like five times. Are you sick?" Brock put his hands on my shoulders and attempted to calm me.

"I . . . I'm not sure what happened. I think I ate something bad, maybe?" Shaking my head, I tried to loosen the fog wrapped around my brain. Something felt wrong, but I had no idea what.

Brock's dark eyes narrowed as he studied my face, and his equally dark brows pinched in a frown. But he didn't say anything. For that I was grateful, but I knew it was only a momentary respite. Of course, Mom and Dad would hear about it for sure, especially since he was taking me home.

"I think I just need a minute, Brock. Could we sit in Soothing Sips for a bit, get some water, and see if I can shake whatever that was?"

"Sure thing. I need to clean up before closing anyway. Come on, little sister," Brock said gently. Placing his arm around my shoulders, he guided me back with him.

Frowning, I couldn't understand what was wrong with me. Did I have food poisoning or was I reacting to something else? But if so, what?

My hands shook. I couldn't stop the tremors. Hiding them in my pockets so Brock wouldn't see, I let him guide me into the small storefront we used in town right next door to Sanguine Elixirs. We partnered with the liquor store to sell our wine and specialty drinks, including an exclusive line for the supernatural population. Because my family was in the business of wine, I knew a lot more than most and have tasted more than I should have, as I was still underage. It was tradition in my family to train us up with all the knowledge for taking over the business when we were older. Luckily for us—at least those who were hunters—we lived longer than the average human.

However, most of the men in my family were not hunters, even some of the women ended up simply human, and sadly, we lost them long before those who were hunters. I have no idea why it worked that way, it just had . . . until now. My younger brother Brice was the first male hunter in centuries, and we didn't yet know what that meant, if anything.

Many people didn't realize Soothing Sips was actually a front for an underground—literally—weapons-making operation for the entire town, if needed. Now don't get me wrong, we hadn't needed weapons for quite some time, but they were there and ready for when the Luna Coven decided we needed to defend Havenwood Falls. For example, back a few years, during the Vampire Massacre of 2005—our weapons saved the town from a drug-crazed bloodsucker. For generations, my family had been making specialized weapons, going back to when the first hunters began hunting witches in the 1800s, and since then, they kept up the practice and skills to train generation after generation of Blackstones. Managing the town's weapons stores was one of our many responsibilities.

It may seem ironic hunters would be in charge of making weapons in a town basically run by witches, but it was done with full knowledge and supervision of the Luna Coven. Plus, the wonderful markings we wore from youth subdued our hunting drive. So there was that—at least I thought so.

Another responsibility we hunters bore was to inform the covens if any of the witches practiced black magic. I still wasn't sure how we did that. I was told I would learn all I needed to know during the orientation before my marking ceremony and initiation into adulthood. I was beginning to think I needed to have that talk with my mom.

I looked up to find Brock carefully watching me.

"Are you sure you're all right, Sprite?" he asked, using my nickname from when I was little. He was the only one who still used it.

"Who are you calling Sprite?" I countered with attitude. "I'm not as small as I used to be, in case you hadn't noticed."

He laughed and gestured to the top of my head and where it hit him mid-chest. I rolled my eyes. "Sure, point out the obvious."

"Well, there's not much else to point out." Brock's teasing took a back seat to a more serious expression and tone. "What happened outside, Sprite?"

"I don't know for sure. My arms felt like they were going numb. Then I felt so sick to my stomach. I couldn't stop the maelstrom of evil that needed to forcefully be ejected from my system. And that's where you found me."

His face contorted into an expression of sheer repulsion—probably remembering the image of the state he found me in. "Sounds like food poisoning to me."

I moved the neck of my shirt and pulled it open for him to see. "My back has been itching like crazy today. I think it's just healing, but could you be a big brother and, you know, scratch it?" I growled with frustration, moving my shoulders back and forth.

Brock laughed, but did as he should and looked at the scabbed area first. "Looks agitated and angry. Do you have more salve from the witches?" But then he scratched, and the relief felt so good, I practically purred.

"At home. Addie Beaumont said it wouldn't heal it super fast. That I would have to have some human patience with that part of it, but it should still cut the healing time in half, if not more," I explained.

"Probably going to leave a scar. Sorry."

"No biggie. Not the first time I've been scarred. I'm a tough hunter, remember?" I smiled and winked exaggeratedly at him.

"Yeah, a tough hunter who thinks she's a spider monkey but is really just a klutz," Brock said with a laugh.

"Ha ha, very funny." I frowned. "I'm not usually klutzy. And don't you have work to finish up here so we can go home for dinner?" Reminding him of his duties usually did the trick. Brock was the responsible sibling.

He went to work cleaning up, while I stared into space, thinking about the mixture of hunters and humans in our family. "Brock? Can I ask you a personal question?" I hesitated because I didn't like to bring it up, and we didn't talk about it very often, but I worried about him sometimes.

"Yeah, Sprite?" he consented without looking up from where he wiped down the counter and put glasses in the dishwasher.

"Do you ever wish you were a hunter? I mean, does it bother you that you aren't one?"

Brock stilled, then wiped the rest of the counter before he looked up at me with those deep, dark eyes of his.

"Do I wish I was a hunter? No. At times, it's hard for Mom to control the power of the hunter side—she thinks no one sees her suffer, but I do. I hope all the time it doesn't affect you and Brice in the same way." He breathed deeply, then let it out. "Does it bother me I'm not a hunter? Every day." Brock placed the dirty rag in the sink. "I'm different. I stand out like Dad does. Sometimes I doubt my place in the family," he replied honestly. His response was so genuine, I paused, almost forgetting to speak.

"Brock . . . I had no idea you felt that way. I wondered, but you've never said anything that straight up about it before."

"No one's ever asked. Well, Dad has, but I figure he had to."

"I'm sorry, Brock. I'll be more sensitive." I reached toward him for a hug. He pulled me in tight and kissed the top of my head.

"Don't change, Sprite. I don't want to be treated any differently than your brother. Just wanted to be honest with you. Now it's your turn."

Uh-oh, not sure I liked where this was going.

"Are you experiencing hunter symptoms early?"

I thought for a minute. "I don't think so, but Mom hasn't given me the entire 411 on what I need to know—though lord knows she keeps telling me I have to get ready for my ceremony. I'm just not ready yet."

He watched me longer than necessary, but I knew he didn't have any "extra" gifts to see with beyond his human eyes. However, he did have brotherly intuition. "All right, but you need to talk to Mom. Deal?"

"Deal," I replied, thinking of what Gallad's mom had said to me earlier. Why was everyone so worried about me? There hadn't been a witch hunter attack in Havenwood Falls as far as I was aware. I didn't feel any need to assault anyone, and my boyfriend was a witch!

"I'm finished. Let's go home." Brock pulled me out through the back of Soothing Sips, which had another door leading down to a secret display room in the cellar below where we stood. He locked all the doors, and we went out the back to his shiny black 1968 Pontiac Firebird. He had a magical silencer put on the muffler so he didn't break sound ordinances inside the town, but it still roared to life when he turned the ignition, and I loved it.

CHAPTER 5

The town wasn't so big I couldn't walk from one end to the other—and I've enjoyed that walk from time to time—but when we drove, it felt like it took only seconds to get from the center of town to our house. Once exiting the square, we headed straight up Eighth Street, crossed Blackstone Road, and began the climb at slow intervals. We arrived at the big metal security gate bearing the words Havenwood Heights. With the click of a control button, Brock opened the gate, and we rolled slowly through it. Havenwood Heights—or the Heights, as I liked to call it—was the old money part of town. The secluded and exclusive lap of luxury, it was filled mostly with the Old Families, the ones who had descended over time or the ones who literally had been here since 1854, when Havenwood Falls was settled.

The sun had made its retreat behind the mountains to the west, but the lingering colors painted the sky, dusting the tops of the aspen and evergreens bordering each property for privacy—not to mention they were just everywhere in Havenwood Falls. Antique lampposts lined the streets, awaiting the chance to shine bright once darkness had fully fallen.

Over the years, parts of our home had begun to descend into old age. In the last decade, the family had our home updated, mixing old log-cabin style with more modern amenities and architecture, giving it the magical Colorado Mountains touch.

Brock sighed. "I do miss this view. It's not quite the same down in Havenstone."

"You could always move back in," I teased. "I'm sure the parentals would love that . . . and so would we young'uns." I smirked at him and jumped out of the car.

"Being on my own has its own magic, too, don't get me wrong. I'm just saying nothing beats this view."

Our home's entry greeted you with gray stone tiles, warm wood beams, and large pieces of art Brock had painted. It guided you to the heart of our house where we spent most our time—the large great room including the kitchen, dining, and living areas. One of the best features was the wall-to-wall windows, broken up only by thick beams of dark-stained wood. My favorite piece of the room, other than the windows, was the floor-to-ceiling rock fireplace with a wide glass front, topped with a hefty chunk of wood for a mantel.

Brock smiled, admiring the original handiwork of one of our relatives, untouched by the more recent remodel. Other aspects of the home, including the underground weapons area that mirrored the one under Soothing Sips, also remained untouched.

"Where is everyone?" Brock asked. "And I hate to disappoint you, but I don't smell anything cooking in the kitchen."

Frowning, I realized he was right. I didn't hear anyone. "Where are they? Tonight's taco night, right?"

A car door shut, and the clacking of heels swiftly arrived at the front door before it swung open, revealing my mom. Confident and powerful, she carried in a large square box, giving off a most delicious aroma.

Upon her arrival, a warmth hummed under the skin at my neck. My hand found its way to the scabbed section but jerked back—it was hot to the touch. My stomach suddenly unsettled again, I lost my appetite.

"I have pizza from Napoli's!" Mom headed straight to the dark gray, granite kitchen bar.

"Mom? Don't we have family dinner tonight? What's going on?" I stood by Brock, both of us just watching, at a loss to what was happening.

She finally looked up at me and cocked her head. "Didn't your father call you?"

We both shook our heads.

"Oh. Well, too late now. I had a meeting come up, and your father ended up having a late meeting at the vineyard." She paused thoughtfully. "Brock, I'm sorry. He was supposed to tell you, so you could make other plans. There's more than enough. Brice should be home soon."

"Sure, Mom, I'll stay for pizza." Brock patted his stomach. He walked over and wrapped his arm around our mom's shoulders. She paused for a moment and relaxed into his embrace.

"You and your father have a way of bringing me a calm when I feel it least." She patted his cheek as he let her go. Then her eyes found mine and narrowed. "Something happened today. What's wrong?"

No, my mom was not psychic—at least not that I knew of—so either she had some mom voodoo going on or Ronya had called her.

"It was nothing, I think my injury is irritated, and I might have food poisoning. I got sick in the square today, and I still feel a bit queasy." I didn't mention the warmth at my neck, growing even hotter the closer she came. She watched me with those mom eyes, but turned her head as soon as the front door opened again.

"Mom? I'm back!" shouted my fifteen-year-old brother, Brice, while he propped his skateboard by the front door.

"In the kitchen," I yelled back at him and took note that the tingling in my neck increased. Brice was adorable in a nerdy kind of way—a cross between a stylish skater and a computer geek with his shy tendencies and thick-framed glasses. And he was the only male hunter we knew of, which made him kind of rare.

"I'll be late," Mom said, grabbing her purse in a hurry. "Macy, we need to talk about your upcoming birthday and ceremony. No more delays. We'll make time the day after the parade." I nodded. The chat was inevitable and maybe even necessary now more than ever. "Brice, in bed by eleven. Macy, you still have to register for your classes or you may not get the ones you want. The information is on the counter." She gave me a stern look, underscoring the seriousness of her message.

"Fine. I'll do it tonight." Resigned, I grabbed the Havenwood Falls High stationary with a blue and silver dragon on it that read "Registration Information" as the subject line.

"Good night, Blackstone children." Mom left, her heels clacking on the tile once more on her way out the door.

As soon as she was gone, the strange feelings at the base of my neck receded drastically. I sighed with relief. A low buzz remained, but it was easily ignored. If it didn't go away on its own, I would have to bring it up.

After we devoured all the pizza, Brock left, and Brice went to play video games in his room. I was left with the damn paper staring at me, taunting me to pick classes for the coming school year—my senior year. After not receiving a reply to the text I sent Ruby, I went ahead and began registering before I picked up the house phone and called her. Cell coverage was spotty in Havenwood Falls, whether from being up in the mountains or too much magical energy interfering or a combination of the two.

"Stupid cell coverage. I tried to send you the same text like ten times. So sorry, but you'll get flooded with texts next time you get reception." Ruby's irritated but friendly voice floated across the line.

"No worries, I know it sucks. Did you register for classes?"

"Yep. My mom already registered for me." Her voice grated with true irritation now. "How's that for over-parenting? I don't know if I can change any of them, but we can go over it if you want."

I laughed. There wasn't much else to do. "Damn. Okay, tell me what classes you have, and I'll see if they are ones I need to graduate."

"Okay, so looks like I've got history with you and Serena and Viv for fourth period with Ms. Bast so far. She's new. I wonder what kind of teacher she'll be," Ruby added.

"I know! I heard she's from Egypt. That should be interesting. Oh, and I'm so excited to ski for PE again!"

"Oh shoot! I'm sorry, I gotta run, Macy. You'll be at the eclipse shindig I planned after the big float reveal tomorrow, right?" Ruby interrupted.

"Yeah, I'll come straight from work so I'll be a little late," I said absently, looking over my work schedule. "You said the float was finished, right? So I don't have to do much else for it?"

She laughed. "Your family is the sponsor of the prize this year *and* the founders of the parade. Do they know you hate the floats?"

"I don't hate the floats—at least not totally—just building them. I have no problem watching them float by me, though, while I sit on a bench with an ice-cold latte or a bag of popcorn."

"Count me in! That sounds divine. Although, I admit I like the idea of riding on one. Okay, gotta go!"

I hung up, shaking my head. Ruby, Gallad, a few other kids from school, and I had joined together to form a team. I was really only on it because my parents told me I had to represent, but I didn't see them out there building a dumb float. We'd been building our monstrosity of a float in one of the old grape-press rooms on the vineyard property—that was my main contribution.

Just as I settled in my room for the night with my latest book, my phone buzzed on the nightstand beside my bed. It buzzed again and again and again. I reached over to it and saw the multitude of texts from Ruby finally come through. I couldn't help but laugh because they were quite intense and irritated. I could hear her practically shouting at her phone through the texts. Then the final text came through, but it wasn't from Ruby. It was from Gallad. Even though it was a stupid text, my heart practically beat through its cage.

G: Hey Macy, just thinking of you. How are you?
   Me: Hi! Good. Reading. You?
G: Wishing I was with you *kissy winky face emoji* (lol)
   Me: awww <3
   Me: Will I see you at the eclipse party tomorrow?
G: I'll be there! I bet you'll be cute in those protective glasses ;)
   Me: lol. See you then! Good night, Gallad.

G: G'night Macy. You know you're my world right?!
Me: *blushing emoji* And you are mine. See you tomorrow.

LAYING BACK ON MY BED, I shifted from one side to the other while I looked up information about the eclipse and the new moon tomorrow. Apparently, it could be seen in the late morning over Colorado. I got off work just as it started, so at least I wouldn't miss it.

"Grrr! This itching is driving me crazy!" I jumped up and put more salve on my back where the healing scabs were, but couldn't reach it all. I was so not waking up my little brother to put it on. Maybe I *should* have it looked at again. Feeling responsible about my decision, I prepared for bed and turned out the lights. Dreams of darkness surrounded me with images of witches surging through it—weaving spells around me, hunting me, provoking me, angering the hunter within me until I lashed out. Free . . .

Reawakened at last.

CHAPTER 6

*M*y morning at Broastful Brew had flown by, but I couldn't help how distracted I was after my night's dreams. I couldn't shake the intensity of the magic that had assaulted me through them. It felt dark, leaving me with a sick feeling in my stomach similar to what I felt yesterday before I hurled in the square. I knew last night was simply a case of bad dreams, but man, they shook me. I woke up drenched in my own sweat, trembling with the exertion of running from the witches, which was backwards since I would be the one chasing them, if I'm the hunter, right? Not that I would. I had no issues with the witches—at least, the ones from Havenwood Falls.

Walking up Thirteenth Street, I headed toward the vineyard. Small decorative evergreens, accompanied by large barrel planters filled to overflowing with colorful flowers, bordered the parking lot. A slight breeze tickled the aspen leaves, delighting the senses with soft pleasing sounds.

As I dodged through the winery, the large building used to create the float came into view. A group of teenagers had gathered off to the side, where I could see Ruby handing out protection glasses for the eclipse. She threw one to new guy Rylan Gilles and tossed several to Will "Kase" Kasun, who handed them out to his usual wolf pack posse. Viv Freeman,

31

Zara Shannon, Aurelia Petran, and several others were there too. So many faces—Ruby had gone all out gathering friends old and new from both schools.

Suddenly, a wave of agitation hit me, causing me to stumble. I sucked in a great breath. Tingling shot up my arms and straight into my heart. I had to stop and clutch my chest. Breathing hard, I couldn't help but wonder if I was having a heart attack.

"Macy, dear, are you all right?" I vaguely heard Aunt Letti's voice penetrate through the fog engulfing me. Strangely, as she approached, I felt a different feeling start at the base of my neck, though this one was more of a familiar warming sensation compared to what I felt the previous night. What was happening?

"I . . . I'm not sure. Can teenagers . . . have . . . heart attacks?" I huffed out, trying to regain my breath.

"Well, I don't know about that, dear. Come sit down and catch your breath while we figure this out." She tugged me by my arm over to a bench in front of the NamaStays Inn main cabin, next to a hand-lettered chalkboard sign advertising "Yoga in the Vines" with the times of the next classes. Aunt Letti was in charge of the bed and breakfast and oversaw the yoga classes. "Sit and enjoy the beauty of the vines and the fresh mountain air. You do have my flair for the dramatic, I fear."

Aunt Letti to those who knew her well—Letitia Blackstone to those who didn't—was my grandmother Eva's cousin, but they couldn't have been more different. Average in most ways, round in the middle—Letti didn't participate in the yoga—with wavy, reddish-blond hair that hung to the middle of her back, Aunt Letti really was the life and spirit around the B&B. Where Grandma was classy and pretentious, Letitia was casual and unassuming, yet they were quite close. I supposed when you outlived most of your family members, you embraced those who remained even more, differences and all.

Aunt Letti kept her gaze trained outward at the new crop of grapes soaking up the sun. We boasted high-altitude crops, though sometimes we used a bit of magic to ensure a harvest during the coldest parts of the growing season. Patting my back in a soothing fashion, she helped me calm down. She casually glanced at me from time to time, but seemed to know watching me would make matters worse. After a few moments, I was able to inhale normally again. I sucked in a deep rush of air and slowly let it out.

"Thanks, Aunt Letti. I think I'm better now. Must have been a panic attack or something," I rambled out something ridiculous.

Her eyes narrowed slightly, taking all of me in, but she smiled and nodded. "Don't kid a kidder, dear. I bet the power of the eclipse was overlooked when the injury to your marking was evaluated." Her gaze, full of wisdom and keen observation, pierced directly into my eyes. "You should go home, Macy. Talk to your mother."

"I'll be okay, Aunt Letti. I can't miss the eclipse!" I jumped up.

"The eclipse has begun, and your reaction will only intensify as the moon advances."

I gave her a quick hug, noting the warmth at my neck surged at the closer proximity. "Be careful, Macy, with yourself and your friends," Letti warned before I dashed away.

Instead of heading into the gathered group of eclipse watchers, I jogged to the building to check out our finished float for tonight's parade. As I moved away from Aunt Letti, the warmth behind my neck receded, but the tingling in my arms remained. In fact, it grew stronger. Shaking my hands, I attempted to rid myself of the feeling, to no avail. The warmth at my neck, I realized, happened only around my family members—except not at Soothing Sips with Brock—meaning only hunters. As for the tingling, I still wasn't sure.

The smells of aging wine hit my senses, and I breathed deeply. It was in my family, in my blood. The smells of the wood oak barrels soothed something deep in me, which was one of the reasons we originally entered the wine business—to calm and soothe the inner hunter.

"There you are!" Ruby yelled, coming in behind me. "I've been waiting for you. You have to see the finished product!" She grabbed my arm and pulled me along behind her. "Ta-da!" Ruby announced with arms flung wide, before a monstrosity of a float transformed into a beautiful spectacle.

"Wow! It looks great!" I admired the float. "Being the new moon tonight, will anyone see it, with how dark it will be?" I asked, eyeing the star decorations.

"Oh, Macy, that's the best part!" Ruby clapped her hands. "The stars all have LED lights behind them, see . . ." She plucked one off the cloud-like bottom of the float and turned it over so I could see the tiny lights. Then she turned her beaming smile toward me.

"I love it. That will look great at night!" I couldn't help but be a little excited about what they had done.

"I can't believe the parade is tonight! I'm so excited to see it lit up!"

"It should be magical," I agreed. "Speaking of magic, when does the eclipse peak, Ruby?"

"Oh! Anytime now," she said excitedly and pulled me outside. Ruby raced around, handing out glasses to anyone she'd missed, before she came back and placed some in my hands, too.

I laughed at Ruby's exuberance.

The rest of the group gathered out by the fire pit while I hung back by the barn. Catching my eye, Gallad smiled and waved as he moved closer to me. My arms tingled more intensely than ever. Clenching my fists, I did my best not to react, but failed. Gallad's eyes narrowed on me. He grabbed my hand with his. I flinched. I didn't mean to, but he took me by surprise. The area between his eyes puckered as he frowned. "You all right, Mace?"

"Little tired from work this morning, I guess. It was busy." I gently pulled my hand away from his touch, from the sizzle where my skin burned against his. I could see the hurt in his eyes, but also something else.

"My mom said she felt something yesterday when she ran into you," he whispered.

"She told me."

"She was worried about you." He placed his hand on my shoulder, but everywhere he touched me, agitation surged underneath my skin. I needed space.

"I think she was more worried about you, actually," I mumbled.

"I'm worried about you." His words were soft and sincere. Gallad's brows pinched momentarily, but he let whatever he wanted to say slide for the time being, making the conversation seem as natural as possible.

Needing to change the subject, I put the glasses on and looked up to the sky. As the moon moved, daylight faded slowly, like it would as it neared evening. The protective glasses kept me from seeing anything other than the round black orb moving in front of the sun. As suddenly as the agitation had hit me earlier, now a surge of energy shot through my arms. My hands flexed and fisted against the pain.

"Gallad, I'm sorry, but I need to go home." I hesitated, but took my glasses off to see his face. His expression gripped my heart. You'd think he lost his puppy. "Don't worry, I'll be fine, you'll see." I forced a smile, a feeble attempt to convince him and possibly even myself.

"No, Macy, talk to me. What's going on?" Leaning his head close to mine, he tipped my chin up with his free hand and stared deep into my eyes.

Breathing slowly through the pain, I held myself perfectly still, all sensations bottled up and contained for the moment. I couldn't let my guard down even for a second.

As if reading my thoughts, Gallad spoke to my heart. "I would never fear you, Macy Marie Blackstone. I trust you. I know you. Do not for a second pull away from me. I see the fear in your eyes. It's looking for a place to control you. Don't let it."

He always had a way with words. They reached into my soul and anchored themselves there, knitting together with the fibers of my being. I let out a slow breath. "I didn't want to admit what might be happening, but I might be losing control of my hunter. Somehow the magic on my tattoo isn't holding. I don't want to lose you, Gallad. I was afraid they'd keep me away from you," I admitted quietly.

"Ooh! Look! The moon is almost all the way in front of the sun!" Ruby's happy voice floated to me from one side. I put the glasses on and looked up to see the eclipse. The sight was amazing, but my attention tore away as something sharp stabbed me from the inside out. I gasped and hunched over. My breaths shortened. I felt on the verge of a breakdown.

"Gallad!" I started to call to him, but my vision swam and the tingles in my arm ratcheted up to becoming nearly unbearable. I crossed my arms, trying to contain the raw shooting pains. Breathing in and out through my nose seemed to calm me and give me a focus to channel the pain, but it started to move through my entire body.

"Macy?" Gallad asked, suddenly way too close. With his hands on my back, he whispered soothing words in a language I didn't know.

Intense pain not only shot through my arms, but my entire body hurt as a power of some kind rushed through me with great force. I fought for a breath. I reached out, then quickly pulled my hand to my chest. Gallad was too close.

"Get away . . . Gallad, go," I managed to say between gritted teeth and short breaths.

"I'm not leaving you."

"Witches . . . away," I panted the only warning I could manage. I could hear a commotion beyond me, but all was fuzzy in my head except for a blasted high-pitched ringing sound. The only thing I could focus on was not acting on my overwhelming urge to hurt Gallad. I refused. I couldn't hurt him; I loved him.

"You're reacting to him, as a witch, aren't you?" Ruby spoke with a hushed tone, coming up next to me, too. More people drew closer as the edge of consciousness faded from my tenuous grasp.

"I . . . can't . . . stop . . ." Curling in on myself, I crouched to the ground, covering my head protectively with my arms. A keening, wailing sort of sound pierced my hearing, but I quickly realized it came from me.

"Macy, look at me." Gallad's soft dulcet tone attempted to draw me back to him, out from the dark hole I crawled into. But as soon as he added magic to his words, all hell broke loose.

I lunged at him like some kind of possessed wildcat and knocked him down to his back.

"Macy!" he shouted at me, but his voice sounded fuzzy and distant.

I didn't have a weapon, so I used fingernails and fists. The sounds of his grunts and hisses told me I landed some hits. His arms protected his face, but otherwise he didn't do much to stop me.

"Macy, stop!" Ruby cried, pulling at my shoulders. "You have to stop!"

"Macy, I love you." Gallad's pained words shot straight to my heart, thinning the haze over my mind and body. Suddenly I could see what I had done.

"Gallad." I could scarcely whisper his name; disbelief, guilt, and horror laced that one word. "What have I done?"

I scrambled off him and away as fast as I could. Panic surged through my being. I couldn't breathe.

I looked up to find the eyes of all my friends trained on me. Disorientation set in. I reached out for the wall and barely found it before I would have fallen over.

Gallad jumped up off the ground, barely even injured. He held his hands out for me. "Macy, let me help you to the inn."

His eyes were not full of hate, but love. How could he even look at me, let alone like he loved me?

"No!" I shouted at him and scooted as far away as I could without falling away from the wall. His head reared back in shock. "I'm sorry, Gallad."

I couldn't explain. I shook my head, and tears slipped from the corners of my eyes. Breathing labored, I felt the world closing in on me, suffocating me from the inside out. I had to leave, to get out of there. Steadying myself, I ran.

"Macy!" Gallad and Ruby both yelled after me.

I sprinted through the vineyard, cutting across the fields at the base of Mt. Alexa toward the backside of Havenwood Heights. I needed to run, to shake off the remnants of what I felt. I needed to feel the freedom of nothing but the breeze through my hair and hear the splashing of the falls in the distance.

I wasn't prepared for this. I was becoming the hunter I wasn't ready to be, and for the first time, I was afraid.

37

CHAPTER 7

*a*t the back of my house, I closed my eyes and let the magical energy of the falls seep into me. I could always hear the falls pretty clearly from my house. After a few moments, I felt strong enough to head inside. With no one home, I slid into the mud room and ran through the house to my bedroom.

Leaning over, I panted to recover from my winded state. My heart pounded so hard, it felt like it was going to explode through my chest. The squishy gray and pink tufted comforter was practically calling my name to come back to bed and snuggle under the thick blankets, to go back to sleep and start this day over again. *If only*. Sighing, I walked toward my desk in front of large windows with a view of Havenwood Falls below me.

"Oh, Marie, I've let you down. I've let my family down. And I let myself and my boyfriend down." My heart broke as I said the words out loud to the woman in the picture frame on my desk. Taken at the turn of the century, it showed my grandmother Eva, great-grandmother Rhea, Aunt Letti, her mother Janella, and Rhea and Janella's mother Marie Marcella Blackstone—my great-great-grandmother and founding member of the Blackstone family in Havenwood Falls—right before she died. I often talked to her. I wasn't sure why, but something about the knowing twinkle in her eye and the slight grin of her lips made me comfortable, like she understood me or what I was going through.

I stepped out onto the balcony, and the instant I did, I felt it—something different than what I had felt earlier with Gallad. A toxic and nefarious feeling overwhelmed me and made me want to vomit. I held my breath and fled back into the safety of my room, shutting the door and the dark feeling out behind me.

"What the hell was that?" I gasped as I fell back on my sturdy bed with thick log beams at the foot and the head. Nope, lying there wasn't going to cut it. I jumped up and ran into my attached bathroom to empty whatever I may have had in my stomach into the toilet.

"Oh, that is not good," I moaned, slurping water from the sink to rinse my mouth out. *Bleh*. The feeling reminded me of the dark feeling from my dream. *Black magic*. The thought flitted through my mind. Black magic was illegal here in Havenwood Falls. Who would dare to practice it and why?

"Macy Marie Blackstone! Are you here?" My mom's voice shouted angrily, shocking me out of my discovery that someone might be using black magic. Other voices joined with hers and wafted up to me from downstairs in the main entry foyer. I froze.

"Oh shit," I whispered, looking around frantically as if there was anything in the bathroom that could help me. "I'm in trouble."

Basic instincts took over. I scurried through my room, grabbed my empty backpack off the floor, threw in some clothes, ran back into the bathroom for my toothbrush, then back out to my desk. I scribbled something quickly on a notepad, a note to my family.

MOM AND DAD,

Something happened. I attacked Gallad. Gallad! I didn't mean to, but I'm not ready for what it may mean. I need some time to myself. I'll be back when I can think clearly. I'm sorry. I love you.

Macy

P.S. I think I felt black magic, but I'm not sure.

THE VOICES DOWNSTAIRS seemed to be growing impatient. I listened as my mom offered tea and cookies. Their feet shuffled from the entry into the main part of the house. Stealthily, I snuck out of my room to my parents' room, but stopped at the door. Several feet away from their door was the family library. I quickly moved in that direction and peeked my head inside. When no one stirred, I ran in, grabbed a specific book off the shelf closest to the mantel, and shoved it in my bag. Back at Mom and Dad's door, I slipped inside.

"I thought I heard something. I'm sure I felt her upstairs. Please make yourselves comfortable and excuse me. I'll go and get her." Lilith's voice echoed from the kitchen.

Quickly, I moved through their large master bedroom to a door leading to a much larger back balcony with a staircase down to the ground level. I couldn't even explain why I was leaving, except I couldn't face what I had done yet. I hated being a hunter right then. All I wanted was to be normal for even one day, to see beyond the mountains, to not feel like everyone was watching me, waiting for me to screw up or attack a witch—and now I had! One or two days of freedom from the awful humming in my body so I could think was all I needed.

Decision made, I jumped down half the flight of stairs and took off at a dead sprint. The exhilaration took hold of me, and the rush of the fresh air and the knowledge of my forthcoming freedom caused a giddiness to bubble out of me. I ran as quietly as I could all the way down to Blackstone Road, which would curve along the outskirts of town, leading down to the main exit, Country Road 13 aka Burdorf Pass. Once I started to slow down so as not to be too conspicuous, but then I would feel it—the tingling up my arms, into my chest. My mom never talked about having these types of feelings as a hunter. It must have been because of the injury to my tattoo, or maybe some kind of punishment. Or maybe I was simply broken. Instead of Brock being the one who didn't fit into the family, it was me all along. Somehow I always knew it would be me.

I ran again, not wanting to feel, not wanting to hurt, not wanting to be afraid.

At the edge of town I stopped, attempting to catch my breath. I had never been beyond this point, and my nerves flared up.

"Is this a mistake? What will I do once I get down the mountain?" I asked myself. "I'll figure it out, that's what. I'm resourceful and smart. I can do this. Besides, it's only a couple days. No worries."

I felt fearless already. I sucked in a huge gulp of courage and took the first step. When lightning didn't strike, I took another step. There was quite a distance still before reaching the actual boundaries of the wards around the town, but my mark kept a tighter control on me than most.

I took one last look back at my little town, my home. It was time for me to stretch my wings a bit.

As I took the final step over the immediate boundary—the road into town—Havenwood Falls was literally behind me. I thought I heard my name being called, but it was only in my head. Now, as my own determination grew stronger, the tangible fear lessened with each step I took. The next thing I knew, I was running down the gradual decline of the mountain road. I ran. And I ran.

Slowing to a walk after some time passed, I rested a few moments and paused to admire the nature surrounding me, from the forest trees on either side of the paved road to the ferns and ground-covering plants to the smallest flowers poking through the rough forest floor. It amazed me how they survived with even the smallest glimpses of sunshine. The sun would go down soon, and underneath the tree canopy it would grow darker earlier. Even though it was summer, in the mountains the evenings cooled very quickly. I untied my heavy sweatshirt from around my waist and put it on. Wishing I had grabbed a bottle of water from the shopping center before I left town, I decided to slow my walk to conserve energy. I didn't actually have time to look at a map, so I didn't know exactly how far it was to the bottom, especially on foot.

A rumble came from behind me, and I froze. What kind of animal made a rumbling noise? I racked my brain, until finally the large bus used to bring tourists and guests up and down the mountain with a big sign for Havenwood Falls moved around the corner I had rounded seconds before. It slowed when the driver saw me and pulled over as much as he could on the narrow road and still leave room beside him—for who I didn't know. It wasn't like traffic was abundant on this road.

The driver, whom I didn't recognize, climbed out of the bus and gave me a friendly wave. He eyed me suspiciously, but shrugged it off. "Hello, miss, would you be needing a ride down the mountain? It's a long ways yet, and I've got room for ya."

I thought about it for all of two seconds, and the idea of saving my feet persuaded me. "That would be really nice, thank you."

"Well, come on then. I've got a schedule to keep." He winked at me, then got back in the bus. I hurried behind him.

"Thank you," I said as I passed him.

Heavily cushioned seats sat two to each side of the center aisle. I took the first empty row, which thankfully happened to be a few from the front. I wouldn't mind chatting with the driver on any other occasion but I didn't feel like explaining why I was obviously underage and leaving in a hurry. The bus was far from full, but a few other people filled some seats. Thankfully, all the strange sensations circulating through my body had found peace and quiet. Perhaps so could I.

I STRETCHED and yawned after stepping out of the bus once we had stopped. I couldn't imagine having to walk the entire way down the mountain. And thankfully, I picked the best time of year to take an out-of-town adventure so we didn't have to deal with extreme weather conditions. According to the bus driver, I was in Durango. The several hours' drive seemed like forever, and evening had fully fallen. Back home, they were about to start the Parade of the Perseids. Looking up, I hoped to see some of the meteors falling, but there was too much light down here in this part of town. Sadness fell upon me when I thought of not saying goodbye to Ruby and the others. I couldn't even think about what I did to Gallad.

I needed to find somewhere to spend the night. The bus driver had pointed in the direction of restaurants and accommodations for those of us who chose to stay in Durango. A motel would be my first stop, then food.

Finding a quaint little inn proved to be easier than I had thought. At first, the clerk didn't want to rent me a room as I appeared underage. She was a sweet, plump older woman who seemed like one to fuss over everyone. However, after I pointed out it was safer for me that she give me the room and knew where I was than for me to be wandering the streets, her last resolve broke. I paid with the cash I borrowed from my parents' emergency fund hidden in the book I'd grabbed from the library.

I settled into my room and decided it was too late to go get food in an unfamiliar town, so I raided the vending machine for snacks. The inn had a continental breakfast, and in the morning, I'd stock up before I hit the town. But tonight I would allow the sadness and guilt of what I'd done drown me into sleep.

CHAPTER 8

*W*aking up far from home, I felt as if a weight had been lifted from me. It was like coming up for much-needed air or emerging after a long sleep from a cocoon. Stretching my arms, none of the tingling or sensations of dark power flowed within me. As I thought of Havenwood Falls and my parents, I felt a pinch of guilt in my chest. If I had hurt Gallad, I wouldn't be able to live with myself.

After breakfast, I gathered what food I could and stored it in my room, then hit the street. At first, exploring the small town of Durango was exciting and everything was new. I started to check my cell phone, but stopped myself. I was sure Mom or Dad—or Gallad or Ruby, for that matter—had left messages. I turned it off when I left Havenwood Falls so they couldn't talk me out of leaving. This was something I had to do; I knew it deep down. Sighing, I glanced at the phone still held in my palm and put it back in my pocket. They could wait a little while longer.

Friendly people caught my eye and smiled as I passed by their storefronts and fruit stands near the corner. Families walked hand in hand. A street performer mimicking a silver tin man stood at one corner, and a young man played a guitar at the opposite corner. Many signs and shops promoted the local museum and railroad paraphernalia. As the day went by, I had become familiar with the lay of the land, at least in my little section of Durango.

Sitting at a little café with an outdoor seating area, pondering my next move and what I would do tomorrow, I noticed a girl a little older than me standing across the street. As soon as I caught her eye, her lip curved up sardonically like she was waiting for me to notice her, then she turned and went the opposite direction down the crowded sidewalk.

"Wonder what her issue is?" I said out loud to myself, barely noting the warm sensation crawling down my neck.

Having eaten my dinner, it was fun to simply sit and watch people. After a little while, I couldn't keep the guilt at what I had done to my parents away any longer. Of course, I could have handled all that had been going on with me better. But at the time, with all the new feelings I had been experiencing, I couldn't think straight. I was in for some big trouble when I went home. I stared at my phone like it would bite me, and perhaps it would with all the messages about to flood through it when I powered it on. Well, no time like the present to rip off the Band-Aid. I turned it on. After a second, it buzzed with text after text, then voicemail after voicemail—mostly from my family, and even one from Brice, which surprised me. I listened to his first.

"Macy, Mom shut herself in the library today, muttering how it was all her fault. I don't know what all is happening, but come home now. Your momentary show of rebellion or whatever this is needs to end. And we're worried about you . . . okay, even I'm worried about you. It isn't like you to just leave." Brice hung up.

"Sprite, what the hell? You have no idea what it's like out there on your own. I'm worried about you. Mom's going nuts in her not-speaking-hiding-in-her-room way. Dad's got a search party getting ready to come look for you. Hurry back before the ward's effects start to mess with your—" Brock's message was cut-off as the call dropped. I'm pretty sure he was going to say mind. We were taught early on that without special permissions and arrangements from the Luna Coven, if you were outside the town's boundaries for more than a moon's cycle, roughly twenty-eight days, then you would lose your memories of the town and its location. I wouldn't be able to get home if I wanted to. Well, I'd only been gone one day so far, so I was pretty sure I didn't need to worry yet.

The next message was from Ruby. She yelled at me to get my butt back to Havenwood Falls, adding that Gallad was fine and didn't blame me. Even though it made me laugh, it hurt my heart to hear her voice, so I skipped on to the next message from Dad. He also yelled at me to call home and tell them where I was so he could come get me. I could hear the fear and worry in his voice. I hated that I put that there. My resolve started to fail. *I should go home.* I had proven I could leave town on my own.

The message I had been skipping, the one that meant so much to me, sat waiting to be heard. Gallad. I'm sure my disappearance hurt him deeply. I was a coward. I attacked him, then couldn't even face him. Instead, I ran. Suddenly I couldn't stomach hearing his voice, the guilt weighing heavily upon my heart. My food sat like a stone in the pit of my gut.

I paid my bill and headed down the road. I wanted to walk a bit more before turning to head back to my room for the night. It dawned on me my mom had not left me a message. Did she think since everyone else did, she didn't need to? Shouldn't hers have been the first one on there? I mean, I knew she raised me to be fully independent and capable even at a younger age, but still . . .

My mother loved me. I knew she did. But at times, she seemed more caught up with her seat on the Court, the vineyard, and her own frailties from being a hunter that perhaps she thought her job as my parent was finished. Or maybe she was mad at me for not letting her tell me all I should have already known by now.

Sighing, I saw a flash of long blond hair fly around the corner up ahead of me. The same feeling of warmth spread down the back of my neck like it did before.

"I thought these feelings would be gone once I was away from Havenwood Falls," I mumbled to myself. I must have been wrong when I associated that feeling with proximity to a hunter. As far as I knew, there were no other witch hunters around here.

"Did you say Havenwood Falls, my dear?" a kind, curious voice emerged from an elderly woman as she stepped out of a soaps and lotions storefront. The mix of fragrances wafted out with her. I froze. Outsiders weren't supposed to know about Havenwood Falls.

"I think you may have misheard me," I started to reply.

"I know someone who lives there . . . at least she did. I doubt she lives there anymore," the woman prattled on.

"No, I'm sorry, I don't know," I replied. My head began to hurt, I was so confused. Rubbing the back of my neck, I recognized the same warmth, though not as strong. I saw the flash of blond hair that had disappeared around the corner only moments ago step into a different shop across the street. "Excuse me, ma'am, but I have to go."

"Oh, of course, dear. Don't mind the ramblings of an old woman." Then she did something odd. Reaching out to gently grip my arm, she added with a straight and serious tone, "Don't ignore the feelings. Let them reawaken within you."

Without further explanation, she simply turned and left. For a moment I debated whether to follow her to ask exactly what she meant or to go after the blonde who had been watching me. The blonde won.

It could have been any random blonde woman, but something about this one triggered a reaction in me, and my gut told me to follow her. Only, when I crossed the street and ducked into the store I watched her walk into, she was nowhere in sight.

"Well, that didn't work out, did it, Macy?" I scolded myself. With hands on my hips, I decide to call it a night and headed back to my comfortable little room at the inn.

The next few days went by in a similar manner. I didn't know why I stayed longer than I had planned to, except I kept seeing the girl with the long blond hair right before she elusively slipped past me and out of my sight—almost as if she was taunting me. But I had no reason to believe she would be spying on me, let alone playing some game of cat and mouse with me.

After another failed attempt to sneak up on my mystery girl, I took a break and grabbed a coffee at the little café I had now deemed as my place to hang out. Staring at my phone once more, I chewed my lip and contemplated calling someone from home, perhaps even Gallad. But the longer I was away, the harder it seemed to simply check in and let them know I was all right. *Ugh*. That shouldn't be the case with family and friends, but I felt foolish for my responses and for leaving the way I had. Once I let the messages come through, I turned on airplane mode; it was too overwhelming, and I wasn't ready to be located.

I pulled up a selfie Gallad and I had taken on a day we worked on our float for the parade. We had made goofy faces, but it still made my heart thump erratically to see his gorgeous face so close to mine. Tears sprang to the corners of my eyes and threatened to spill over. The indicating warmth seeped into my back just before I looked up.

"Hello, dearie. From Havenwood Falls, right?" The elderly woman from the other day sat down at a table next to me. "Such a coincidence to meet you again."

She was probably in her early seventies—not that I was any good with guessing ages when most of the people I knew from home were often quite a bit older than they seemed. I smiled, but something niggled in the back of my mind. I didn't believe in coincidences, though she seemed harmless enough to chat with from another table.

"Lovely day today, isn't it?" I asked, making small talk, nodding up at the bright blue skies of the warm August afternoon. The weather had been cooling down quickly at night, but the afternoons remained pleasant.

"Indeed. Are you staying near here, dearie?" she asked innocently enough, but my alerts went on full volume.

"Perhaps. You?" I rebutted in my not-so-subtle teenage way of not entirely caring if it came out rude or not. Fortunately, she simply laughed at my response.

"Touché. I was merely trying to make conversation, I apologize. But yes, I do live near here. This is my favorite part of town. It can be lonely for an older woman these days, and I like to get out where I can watch the people." She pointed at me where I was seated facing the street. "It doesn't look like you are doing much different."

"Touché." I repeated her word and shrugged. She seemed harmless enough, but unless the warmth crawling up and down my spine when I talked to her before and again now—as well as when I was near my family—was also a coincidence, then I had an unknown hunter chatting with me.

"I'm Macy. What's your name?" I decided to go on the offensive and find out as much as I could.

"Nice to meet you, Macy. My name is Grace Blackstone."

She simply waited for me to acknowledge what she had said, but I couldn't. I was frozen internally. Externally, I schooled my features and willed them not to give anything away. How could there be a Blackstone —and a hunter to boot—only hours away, living in Durango? Could this woman be my family? I gulped, possibly loudly. I needed more information.

"How long have you lived here in Durango, Mrs. Blackstone?"

"Not long, actually, maybe a few months. I moved here with my family."

She set me up, I was sure of it. Curiosity may very well have killed the cat, but I was smart—I'd ask a few more questions. It would be responsible of me to gather information to bring to the coven and my family back home.

"Family?" I asked, prodding her to continue. "Is it a big family?"

"Oh, there are quite a few of us Blackstones. Right now I'm out with my niece. I'd like you to meet her, if you don't mind. She's not far."

"Of course, invite her to join us," I offered.

A sneaking suspicion shot through my mind as soon as she mentioned having a niece. *Yep, sure enough.* The back of a blond ponytail rounded the entrance to the café.

"Nala, come meet my new friend. The game is not necessary," Grace supplied as she waved the girl over to her table. I'm not sure "friend" was a word I would have used quite so early in our meeting, but we'd see.

Nala was older, probably in her early twenties, and taller than I had been able to surmise from across the street. Her long blond hair, tied up and pulled away from her face, allowed her striking features to draw all eyes to her. Watching me were large almond-shaped, blue eyes framed with thick, long eyelashes I was instantly jealous of. Flawless skin matched with high cheekbones and defined features added to the badass, Norse goddess vibe she sported. I wanted to be her, and at the same time, I wanted to tell her to relax unless she was late for the movie set.

"Nala, this is Macy. Macy, this is my niece, Nala." Grace gestured with her hand for Nala to sit. Nala nodded but stared at me as if she waited for me to speak first. Fine.

"Nala, I've heard your name somewhere before . . . Oh! I know, it was the name of the lioness from an old Disney movie. Is that who you were named after, for your intense prowess and stalking abilities . . . to hunt?" I asked with a bit too much snark for someone I had newly met, but something about her rubbed me the wrong way. How hard was it to say "nice to meet you"?

An awkward moment passed where Nala stared me down. Then the side of her lip quirked, and a muscle twitched in her jaw. Was she laughing at me?

"I remember hearing something about that movie." She sat down gracefully in the chair across from her aunt, from which she could watch me. In what might have been the only way she could relax, she crossed her legs and folded her arms. "So you're a Blackstone, too?"

My mouth fell open.

"You are, aren't you? There's really no point denying it." She turned to Grace. "Or dancing around it, Aunt Grace. We know. She knows—at least if she's any kind of a hunter, she knows."

"I guess we're not pulling any punches here, are we?" Was this good? Was it bad? I was in unfamiliar territory here.

"No reason to." She picked at a nail she focused on too closely. Apparently reading my discomfort, she added with an exasperated sigh, "Listen, Macy, we just wanted to see who you were and if you posed any threat to us. As long you don't, we can be friends."

"I could pose a threat." Not sure why I got a sudden case of defensiveness. I didn't need enemies right now. *I should back away and run home.* "If I wanted to, I mean. Not that I do," I quickly backpedaled.

Nala laughed, and Grace simply looked at me with an entertained twinkle in her eyes, both obviously humoring me.

"Why do you want to be friends with me?" I asked, suddenly quite suspicious.

"My dear, we're family. Why wouldn't we want to be friends with you?" Grace asked.

Okay, that made sense. Then a thought struck me that I apparently asked out loud. "Why did I not know I had other family out here?"

Nala looked out at the street, then back at me.

"Maybe they didn't know?" she supplied weakly, then shrugged. "Or maybe they didn't think you were ready to know?"

"Well, whatever the reason, we can remedy it now, can't we?" Grace took a sip of her iced tea. She smiled, then looked to me.

"Perhaps. I will be heading home soon, but could we meet for lunch tomorrow?" I asked, needing a little space to think and perhaps even call my parents to tell them I found lost family members.

"That sounds lovely, dear." Grace stood up and grabbed her handbag. Nala also rose from the table.

"Same place?" Nala asked.

"It's a date!" I exclaimed with a little more jubilance than I meant to. Quickly, I felt a pang in my chest with the name Gallad written all over it. I missed him. Apparently it showed in my face.

"Call your young man, Macy. You never know when the next time you might get to speak with him will be. Don't regret it," Grace encouraged, as if from the depths of some place in her heart.

"How did you . . ."

"Know about your boyfriend? I saw you longingly look at a photo when I came over," she explained.

I nodded and waved my phone at them as I left the café, heading to my room for the night.

Maybe I could bring them home with me to Havenwood Falls. Wouldn't that be the surprise of the season!

CHAPTER 9

lmost a week had passed, and I couldn't believe how fast the time had gone by. Guilt swamped my emotions, flooding me with visions of my family, of Ruby, and of Gallad. I missed them all, and I couldn't believe what I had put them through. Everyone had suffered enough, not that I intended for anyone to suffer. My only intention had ever been for me to escape the plague caused by the simplest act of stupidity and a tree.

Walking to the café, I decided to tell my family I was coming home on the next bus out of Durango. My money had almost run out, and I wouldn't have enough to pay for another night at the inn. Perhaps my dad would even come get me. I checked out of my room and filled my backpack with food from the inn's breakfast.

After turning my phone on, I went through the countless text messages once again from Ruby and other friends, these asking if I would be back in time for the first day of school. I looked at the calendar on my phone and realized school was scheduled to start the next day.

"Oh no! I can't miss the first day of school," I muttered out loud. Just as I had said it, my phone chimed—voicemail from my mother. My heart quickened. She had yet to call me. I wanted to hear her voice as desperately as I wanted to slam my phone down and ignore her call altogether. Sighing, I gave in and held the phone up to my ear.

"Macy," her voice began, and with it, a sliver of pain stabbed into my heart. Tears rose in my eyes, but I quickly squelched them back. I paused to lean against a brick building while listening. Mom's voice broke, and for the first time in my life, I heard fear and guilt laced in her shaky words and hesitation. My mom, Lilith Blackstone, matriarch of the Blackstone hunters, was never afraid—or at least never showed it. "Macy, I feel an urgency to tell you . . . I should have told you sooner . . . I put it off, I thought I had more time before your hunter began to reawaken. I didn't prepare you for what you would feel. We didn't understand how the energy from the eclipse would interfere with your healing tattoo. This is my fault. I'm sorry, child. Please come home. I understand, more than I hope you ever know, I understand the drive to run. It's overwhelming, scary, and even painful. Oh, Macy, be careful out there. You needed time. I understand that, too. I tried to get everyone to give you time. Your father has been searching for you, but I know you'll come back when you want to be here." She paused for an uncomfortably long moment, but I could hear her heavy breathing. "Please listen, Macy. Run when you have feelings that make you intensely, toxically sick. That is a witch's black magic. I can tell you more when you get home, but the lesser feelings, usually where your hunter marking is located, tell you when other hunters are nearby . . . And Macy, there may be other hunters nearby." Her volume grew and her pace quickened as if she was suddenly in a hurry. "Other Blackstones have been sighted in the area. They are dangerous. If you run into any of them, stay away from them, Macy. I love you, child. Please call home."

I stood silently stunned. My mother rarely said she loved us. She must have been afraid for me. She seemed afraid of the other Blackstones. But the ones I met seemed nice enough. Well, Grace did. Nala I could see being dangerous, but she hadn't tried anything so far.

Choked up, I didn't think I could speak yet. I texted a family thread to Mom, Dad, Brock, and even Brice. I told them I got their messages and would be home tonight on the next bus out of Durango. I said I was sorry and told them I loved them. Then I texted the same to Ruby, but

Gallad I called. I needed to hear his strong, soothing voice right then. He picked up on the first ring.

"Macy? Is that really you?" He sounded panicked and relieved all at the same time.

"Hi. It's me. Gallad . . ." I paused.

"Mace, are you okay? Where are you? I'll come and get you right now!"

"Calm down, G." I laughed. It was so good to hear his voice. "I miss you."

"I miss you, too. Seriously, can I come get you?" The hurt in his voice broke my heart—hurt I had put there.

"Gallad, I . . . I'm . . ."

"No, you don't need to explain."

"What the hell are you talking about? Of course, I do! I attacked you —the other half of my heart. You tried to help me, but I was a coward and ran away. I didn't understand the feelings overwhelming me, and I couldn't think straight. Gallad, I'm sorry. I . . . I love you." There. I said it. I had never said it to him before now, even though he had said it to me countless times. But I didn't want to be like my mom in the same regard and wait until it was almost too late. Although, that was exactly what I had done. I didn't want to be closed off with my heart—not with Gallad, not ever.

Silence permeated the other end of the line. I was too late. I had ruined my chance with him, and now I didn't know what I would do without him.

"Come home, Macy . . . please." His voice cracked. If I closed my eyes, I could almost reach out and touch him, his voice was so close. His brown shaggy hair, the cocky air about him he would call confidence, the way he held my hands or held me close . . . it all called me back to him, but nothing more than his striking green eyes that held my gaze and instilled the promise of his love.

"I'll be on the next bus out of Durango. I told my parents. I'm coming home," I told him quietly. "Gallad, I am sorry. I hope you can forgive me in time."

"Just come home, Mace." He ended the call, and I stood there solemnly, catching my breath and guarding my emotions before I met my newest family members for lunch to tell them goodbye—at least until I could come back with my parents and introduce them all together. I had enjoyed meeting up with them this week and getting to know them a little.

With a new plan and renewed excitement about seeing my family and Gallad, I held my head high and headed toward the café to meet Grace and Nala. I tipped my head up briefly to feel the warmth of the sun on my face. Today, a light breeze ruffled the ends of my hair and brought a feeling of fresh perspective to my soul. I was going home, and now that I had decided, I couldn't wait to get there. Nothing terrible had happened, and my little getaway proved I could do it on my own in the future.

Spotting Grace and Nala already seated in the outdoor section, I waved when they caught my eye. Both smiled and waved me over to them.

"Good afternoon, Macy." Grace welcomed me. All I got from Nala was a nod and a brief smile. At least she didn't frown at me.

"Hello," I said as I sat at their table. "Did you order already?"

"No, we waited for you, dear."

Taking the menu she held out for me, I looked over it quickly and decided.

"Are you ready already?" Grace asked, with a light chuckle.

"I'm pretty simple. I know what I like. They have a wonderful tomato basil soup and grilled three-cheese and bacon sandwich here. I want to savor it one last time." I sighed gleefully at the mere thought of it as my mouth began to water.

"Oh, I want that now," Nala chimed in unexpectedly. When I raised an eyebrow at her, she shrugged.

"What? It sounds good."

The waitress came by to take our order, then quickly dashed off to her next table of new arrivals.

"Did you say last time, dear?" Grace asked, bringing my attention back to her right as something strange flitted swiftly behind her eyes.

Cocking my head, I didn't hide the fact that I caught it. "Um, yes.

Tomorrow is the first day of my senior year, and I need to get back home. My little getaway has come to an end."

"It has been so lovely getting to know you. I do hope we can see you again," Grace said with a spark of sadness in her eyes.

"Let's just eat and enjoy our last day then," Nala urged, strangely focused on Grace.

"Of course, of course." Grace patted my arm on the table next to her. "Did you have a chance to call your young man, Macy?"

I blushed. "I did."

"Good. Good." She winked at me.

"You had mentioned knowing someone from Havenwood Falls. Who was it? I'm not supposed to talk about it, but I figure since you already know about it, it couldn't hurt." I looked up at her expectantly.

"Yes, it was long ago, but one doesn't forget the connections of family easily. It helped she had come to meet me outside of Havenwood Falls. I suspect there were consequences of some sort, as I didn't hear from her again after that time."

Intrigued, I leaned forward. "Who was it?"

"She may not even still be alive, but she was a cousin of sorts. Letitia Blackstone is her name." Her words exploded in my mind like a dropped bomb. She waited, watching my reaction.

"Well, I can tell you she is still alive. She's my grandmother's cousin. I see her almost every day. I can tell her I met you, and perhaps in the future I can even bring you to Havenwood Falls or bring her here to meet you!"

A spark lit in Grace's eyes; the news seemed almost shocking to her. Quickly she used her napkin to school her features, but it was too late. I saw the longing in her eyes, but for some reason she felt it should not be there or be seen. Seen by me? Or possibly by Nala? I let it go for the moment, but I would try to ask her about it before I left her. Nala eyed Grace curiously as well, but she didn't ask for an explanation either. A strange, awkward silence descended on the table. But then the server brought our meals, and for several minutes, no one said anything while we dug into our food.

"When do you leave?" Nala asked. "And oh wow, this is good. I'm going to have to come back for this again."

"Right?" I beamed, amazed I got her to act somewhat normal for even a mere second. *Score one for me!* "I'll be leaving right after we have lunch. It's a bit of a journey, and I want time to settle back in before school tomorrow."

"Macy, would you be a dear and ask the server to refill my iced tea?" Grace asked, holding out her glass to me. The server would have been back to check on us momentarily, but I didn't want to be rude to my elder, so I took the glass up to the counter to be refilled.

When I returned to the table, there was a sudden tension between Grace and Nala that hadn't been there before I left.

"Everything all right here?" I asked, eyeing them both.

"Of course, dear, thank you for the refill." She took a deep pull from her drink and smiled.

The next half-hour flew by with Grace asking me random questions about myself and about my boyfriend—though I was selective about what information I gave her. Knowing she was from our family of hunters, I wasn't sure of her views on dating a witch. Nala chimed in occasionally, but mostly she stared out at the street.

"We wish you didn't have to go, Macy," Grace finished. "I've enjoyed our time out here, getting to relax at this wonderful café."

"It has been lovely. I hope to see you both again in the future," I replied, even including Nala. Uncharacteristically, she gave me a big wink.

"Oh you will, you can count on that," Nala countered, watching me intently.

"Ok . . . well, I should be going soon." I started to stand up, but my knees felt wobbly, like they couldn't hold my weight. "Whoa, maybe I need just a minute." My head started to spin, and I clutched it tight.

"Are you all right, dear?" Grace's voice came through the fog permeating my brain.

"I . . . I don't know. I don't feel so good." The fog spread thickly in my brain, and fuzziness crept in front of my vision. Was I fainting? That fight-or-flight drive surged in my chest, but my limbs felt like lead. Was I even moving them? I couldn't see. But I could still hear.

"You'll be fine, dear. I'll keep an eye on you," Grace's voice whispered in my ear.

"Let her go, Grace. Dante wants to meet her." Nala's words stuck with me as I tried to process what she was saying. Who was Dante? Why did that name sound familiar?

"Whaz happen . . ." Was that my voice slurring? "I can't fweel ma tung . . ." Seriously, what was wrong with me?

Suddenly, the ground was torn out from under my feet, and the air moved on my face. Was I being carried?

"Get her in the car, boys," another woman's voice echoed in my head. Boys? What boys? Panic bubbled up in my chest, but all I could manage was a groan. What was happening to me? The next thing I knew, I was slipping into darkness. I fought it as long as I could, but the darkness won. As I went under, the last thought I had was of Gallad. I saw his face in my mind, his eyes twinkling when he said he loved me. I felt his tender but firm lips over mine as he kissed me and heard his masculine and confident voice as he said my name. I wanted to go home.

CHAPTER 10

*V*oices penetrated through my brain like rays of light breaking through dense fog with sporadic effectiveness. Sometimes words were recognizable, and other times only indistinguishable sounds hit my brain as I tried to comprehend what I heard. I didn't know if it was days or minutes that passed before I heard a familiar voice cut through the haze.

"Macy, it's time to wake up."

"Mom? Is that you?" I croaked, my voice scratchy and thick. I wasn't even sure what I said was decipherable as words. My cracked lips smacked as I moved my tongue around in my mouth, trying to get it to work properly. Had I been eating cotton? *Yuck*.

"No, dear. Have some water." A glass was put up to my mouth, and I began to slurp down my liquid savior. "Slowly now. You don't want to choke." The voice soothed me as she spoke.

"Am I blind?" Panic started to erupt. I absently patted the space around me.

She chuckled. *Seriously?* I was concerned about being blind the rest of my life, I had no idea where I was or what was happening, and someone *laughed* at me? I growled in response.

"Your vision will slowly return. Don't worry, dear."

"I know you . . ."

"Yes, it's Grace, child." I felt her warm breath closer to my ears as she whispered the next part. "I'm sorry it had to happen this way." She sounded sad.

I needed a minute to breathe, to calm my overactive heart. I couldn't do anything blind. I needed to get my body back under my control. I pushed air in through my nose and out through my mouth. I let the act of breathing help me to gain command of myself. I remembered Grandma Eva instructing me when I was younger. She taught me ways to master not only myself when I felt powerless but also when I felt the drive of the hunter pushing to the forefront. I just wished I had remembered those lessons before I fled Havenwood Falls. Then I wouldn't be in this mess. Suddenly, the memory of my mom's voicemail warning me about other hunters rushed back to me. She was right. I didn't even know entirely why, but something here was very wrong.

The fog lifted from my brain, and the darkness receded from the edges of my sight. Slowly but surely, my vision returned. I just couldn't tell if Grace was on my side or planning to hurt me.

The prison they held me in came into view. I lay on a twin-sized bed in a pink room. The room had a closet full of girl clothes, a desk with books stacked on top of it, an overflowing hamper near the door, and posters of eighties bands and movies. On a chair right next to me sat Grace, her eyes full of concern as she watched me come out of the sleep-induced fog I was battling.

"Grace? Why have you done this?" My voice cracked. Fear crept in. What did she mean the way it had to happen? "Where's my phone?" I patted my pockets but felt nothing.

"We have it, and you will get it back. But until you've heard us out, it's being held in a safe place."

I practically roared, I was so upset. I had been kidnapped by an elderly woman and her ninja Nala posse. How lame was that?

"I need to go home. My parents will come looking for me if I'm not home tonight."

"Sweet child, you have been asleep for a week."

"WHAT?" That was a bomb I didn't know how to recover from. I sat up with a rush, quickly regretting it as I did. "Did you say a week?"

"Slowly, or you will make yourself sick." Grace reached over to pat my arm, but I pulled it back, not wanting her comfort. She had betrayed my trust.

"You said we were family. How could you do this to me?" Anger seethed. I fought my emotions for control. Placing my head on my knee, I tried to regain my balance. The more I allowed my body to recover, the more I felt the warmth bloom behind my neck. The sensation was much stronger than before with Grace—which meant more hunters were present.

Her sigh sounded remorseful, but I didn't care or believe it now. It was too late for remorse.

"I missed the beginning of school." Yes, I pointed out the obvious, but I was still muddled a bit in my head.

"I'm sorry, dear," she whispered. Her head hung low, and she seemed truly sorry. Still no grace for Grace.

"Tell me why," I demanded. Slowly, I raised my head, and I turned my glare on her. I hoped she felt the sting of betrayal in my gaze.

"Because I asked her to." A male voice flowed into the room a second before the body it belonged to followed. A tall, handsome man strode confidently into the room. He appeared in his early sixties, with graying hairs at the sides of his otherwise black-haired head, and was clothed in a gray business suit with even darker gray dress shoes. He had kind of an old Hollywood style about him, but with cold eyes—Hollywood with an edge. His eyes shot to Grace, disapproval striking within them, and I found myself rearing up internally, wanting to protect her even though she betrayed me. What was up with that? *No, she should be on her own*, I thought . . . but maybe she already was.

His steel-blue gaze swung to meet mine. Something dark and malevolent hit me in the chest. I had never encountered anyone with such an intense gaze that it physically assaulted me. Chills erupted up my spine.

"Who are you?" I asked with a bravado I had to pull out of my backside. His lip twitched as if he knew exactly where I pulled it from.

"My name is Dante Blackstone. And I believe you are a member of my family, Macy," he replied. The way he said "my family" did not escape my still slightly fog-addled brain, as if he was the ruler and not just a member of it. It irked me he knew my name. I guessed Grace and Nala were some kind of spies who reported back to this guy.

"Why am I here?" I swung my legs over the edge of the bed, needing to be grounded on the actual ground in case I needed to get up quickly —though I wasn't sure I was physically able to yet.

"Stand down, Macy. I am not planning on hurting you." The side of his mouth quirked up, as if it was funny I thought I had any chance to run or fight at all. "You are here because I have been searching for the rest of my family for a very long time. I wanted the chance to get to know you and for you to get to know us."

"I'd like to go home, please." I hated the whimper I heard in my own voice—like some weakling. I was a hunter, the same as these people, although possibly quite different from them as well.

"Of course. You are not a prisoner here. But you have cousins and relatives who would like to meet you before you do. Would that be all right?" He stood with his hands clasped behind his back.

His way was totally manipulative, but it also worked. Of course I wanted to meet family members. Why wouldn't I?

"It would. It still doesn't explain why I was asleep for a week." The anger surged up once more. *A whole week!* Anything could have happened during that time, and I wouldn't have had a clue. The very thought made me want to throw up, but taking stock of myself, I didn't feel violated in anyway. In fact, I oddly felt stronger the more time went by.

"You have a strength about you, Macy. However, I can tell you have not yet allowed your hunter side to come to the forefront. It has somehow been dampened . . . magically." He said his last word with a tone of disgust accompanied by an ugly sneer. He didn't seem finished, so I remained quiet, though everything in me wanted to lash out with a smart remark. "You see, all those in *my* family are given the freedom to be who they were created to be, to engage in every facet of their being, to awaken the hunter from birth." Those sharp eyes shot directly into my soul. His voice grew in strength as the shadow of something rose up behind his eyes. "Your hunter needs to be reawakened."

"Compelling. Is this where I jump and ask to follow you and remain here with *your* family?" Who did this guy think he was? Slowly, I stood from the bed. I felt Grace move back to allow me space, then inch her way toward the only exit in the room. I didn't blame her. "You took me away from *my* family just so you could see what kind of hunter I could be? Who gave you that right? You have *kidnapped* me! My hunter is just fine, thank you very much. I want to go home. Now."

"We are above the law, Macy. Your hunter called out to us. We deserve our freedom, as do you. They need their freedom."

Oh gag. He talked as if we and our "hunters" were separate beings in the same body. I mean, I've talked about my hunter side, but I'm pretty sure I've never heard my hunter talk to me. Dante paced slowly in a tight circle, as the room hindered his need for space.

"As supernaturals in this world of humans, we have been given the upper hand, the abilities to govern and police our own. It is our responsibility. There are those who have taken liberties to exist outside the *natural* law. Those who conjure and collect the magical elements with a spoken word to do as they will and to harm others. It is our job to govern them. It is unnatural!"

Witches. He was talking about witches, and I did not like the turn this conversation was taking. My skin crawled with a very bad feeling.

"And how do you govern them?" I asked hesitantly, pretty sure I knew where he was going.

Turning to me, his eyes lit up as if excited I was interested in learning his ways. "Excellent question. It is about restoring balance. We remove the unnatural abominations, thus creating a more natural state."

"But don't you think as supernaturals, we are not 'natural' ourselves?" Oops. As soon as I said it, I realized my mistake.

His gaze shot toward me once more. A muscle twitched in his jaw, and another at the corner of one eye gave away his impending anger, but he calmed it quicker than my parents would have. Perhaps he wasn't used to anyone questioning him, or perhaps I hit a nerve.

"We are created to restore the balance. You should know that by your age. Your parents have let your education of our race slide. I can remedy that. Outside of human schooling, those in my family grow up knowing exactly who they are, what they can do, and their position in this world." Holding his hands behind his back once more, he straightened his shoulders—though I had no idea how they could be any straighter—and his facial expression became one of a semi-hospitable host. "I would like to extend the same opportunity to you, Macy. It might take some work at first, but I'm willing to do it."

Gee, don't I feel special. I wanted to roll my eyes so badly, but I refrained and chose my words carefully. "Thank you for the offer, Mr. Blackstone." He smiled and gave a curt and approving nod. Yeah, I could be a suck-up when I needed to be. "But I'm going to have to decline. I can see your family is very important to you, so you'll understand I need to get back to mine. They'll be worried sick and looking for me."

"No need to worry there. We have scouts out looking for them. They will be proud when they see how I have helped you engage your hunter side." Like a peacock, he puffed out his chest as he straightened a lapel.

"I don't think so. They are the ones who agreed to have my hunter tendencies suppressed until I'm eighteen and can choose for myself." Wow. To hear myself speak, I might sound a bit resentful about the fact.

Dante stopped moving and held completely still. Supernaturally still. "They suppress their young, not allowing them to engage with their hunters?"

His voice held a deadly calm, like when the air became electrically charged right before a storm of epic proportions.

"I thought you understood," I said cautiously.

"I thought perhaps you were an anomaly, unable to fully engage," he began matter-of-factly.

"You mean, you thought there was something wrong with me?" I didn't know why that bothered me more than anything else at the moment—maybe because I felt there was truth in it, deep down inside.

"It happens from time to time. All it takes is some kind of trigger to truly engage the hunter, to realign what might be off internally." He shrugged, an unusual action for someone dressed the way he was and carrying himself the way he did. Like a boomerang, he brought the conversation back around. "You were suppressed magically. That leads me to believe you live cohesively with those who do the suppressing? With the magic users?"

"Yes."

Through gritted teeth, he responded. "How can this be? They have gone against their very nature to live in the same community as the witches! I knew long ago my sister decided to fight her hunting urges. She didn't understand the true need for balance, the true cause of our mission. She was misguided and ran from it like a coward . . . But to live with witches . . . to commune with them . . ." He didn't finish his rant. I was done.

"Yep, in fact, my boyfriend is a witch." Why, oh why, couldn't I keep my mouth shut?

"They let you . . ."

"They don't *let* me. I chose him!" I shouted. Gallad was the best thing that ever happened to me, and I wasn't about to let some deranged stranger claiming to be my family belittle that. Okay, so it may have been stupid timing, but whatever.

Dante held his chin high. He breathed in through his nose, held it for a count of three, and then slowly released it again. He appeared to be enacting some kind of control over himself. For that I was grateful, but I was not sorry, and I wouldn't take it back.

"Come, let me introduce you to the rest of your family." Instantly, Dante had flipped a mental switch. This guy was crazy, I was pretty sure of it. But following him would lead me out of this room, and from there I could discover where I was and what I had to work with. Then I would make my move.

CHAPTER 11

*A*fter following the most stoic man ever, with the assistance of my elderly captor, down a long hallway adorned with several doors not unlike an apartment building or hotel, we finally arrived at a large room at one end. Through double doors was a wide-open room with no interior walls, a ballroom at its basest function. This room, however, was full of couches, a large screen television with smaller screens on either side connected to game consoles, an extra-large table with a lot of chairs, and overflowing bookshelves lining one wall. Occupying several seats within the room were roughly ten people. Most appeared younger than fifty, but a few older ones sat at the big table and played cards. When Dante stepped in, the room quieted, and all eyes turned toward him without him even saying anything. The way his presence affected everyone gave me the creeps. Their eyes looked to him first, then fell on me. Mixed expressions surveyed me, but mostly they seemed curious and open.

"Everyone, this is Macy Blackstone. Introduce yourselves and make her feel at home. I have business to attend to and will be back for dinner." He turned to Grace. "Keep an eye on things, Grace."

She nodded and reached out for his arm, but then retracted it. Her face remained in control, but her eyes held sadness. Dante turned on his heel and stopped at me. "Macy, I do hope you enjoy your time getting to know the rest of your family. If you would still like to leave, the morning would be the earliest opportunity, as this evening will be too late to travel. If you wait until the morning, I will escort you home myself."

Seeing my flinch, he quickly amended his words. "Or I would be happy to have Nala or one of the others drive you, if that makes you more comfortable."

I nodded. "I'll think about it."

I had no intention of thinking about it. I would find a way out of here, but I needed to find my phone so I could call Dad to come get me, or at the very least, let him know I was alive. Maybe I could strong-arm —or sweet-talk—Grace into getting it back. She seemed to have reservations about the way they brought me here. I could use that. Dante strode out of the room with great intention. I felt a collective sigh throughout the room, a releasing of the tension as they returned to what they had been doing.

"Macy, come meet some of the others," Grace said, pulling me along by my arm over to the main table where three ladies watched me, not yet picking up their card game again. "Ladies, this is Macy. We're not sure yet how we are related, but she says Letitia is still alive and kicking."

Introductions were made at the table, but honestly, they seemed more interested in knowing about Aunt Letti than anything about me at all. Fine by me; I didn't want to get attached. They had all been very sweet, when I had been expecting animosity—animosity would have been easier. Then I wouldn't think of them like people—or like family I would turn my back on.

Grace then took me over to the couch area where there appeared to be three different video games going on simultaneously. I was dizzy trying to figure out which screen to watch. Brice was a gamer; I played with him sometimes, but never really got into it.

"Macy, this is Sunny, Charlie, and Rachel on the couches." Grace pointed at three different girls about my age. "Girls, introduce yourselves."

"Hey, I'm Sunny." The girl with short blond hair and bright blue eyes and a smattering of freckles on her nose waved with a small smile. She was obviously the youngest.

"I'm Charlie," the girl next to Sunny on the big couch said. Her shoulder-length brown hair with soft waves framed her pale skin, green eyes, and sharp features. She and the other girl, who must have been Rachel, most likely were a bit older than me. She smiled, and her welcoming aura made me relax and think we could be friends. Thinking of friends brought Ruby to the forefront of my mind. I missed her. I hope I got to see her and the others again.

"Hi Sunny, Charlie, and Rachel." I waved, then put my hands in my front pockets, unsure what to do next. I didn't want to be here, making nice with new people, no matter how much I could see familial resemblances in each of them. Rachel lounged in a reclining game chair in front of one of the small screens. She paused her game to look up at me, nodded, and shot me a brief gratuitous smile before returning to her game, which was obviously more important. I didn't blame her. Who was I to her? A random stray brought in off the street. Well, I was not looking to be fed or coddled.

Two boys over on the small couch played their own games.

"Hey, I'm Luke, and this is my brother Jeremiah. We're twins," the one with longer brown hair sweeping across his eyes announced. His twin, Jeremiah, gave me a wave. His hair was cut shorter all around, but other than that, they were practically identical.

"They call us the hunting Houdinis because we're great at disappearing when necessary," Jeremiah chimed in with a chuckle. They couldn't be more than twelve or thirteen. Brice would probably like them. Thinking of Brice . . .

"You both are hunters?" I asked, attempting to hide the surprise in my tone. According to the eyes that all swiveled my way, I failed.

"Of course! Do you see a ghost right now? Because you're kinda pale," Luke said.

"No, but there are no male hunters in my family . . . well, until my younger brother that is." I clamped my mouth shut. I shouldn't have said anything.

"Seriously?" Jeremiah guffawed.

I nodded. Oh well, too late now. Maybe I could find out something about it.

"We have lots in our family," Sunny, the youngest of the girls, supplied. Two other boys, one younger and one closer to my age, were on the floor in bean bags that looked well used. They hadn't been introduced yet, but were quite focused on their game, or at least appeared to be. "Are all your males human then?" Sunny continued.

"Yes, except Aunt Letti—I still have a question on that by the way— she married a dragon shifter awhile back." I heard snorts of disgust from the table behind me, where Grace had sat herself down. I turned with an eyebrow raised in question. "Care to comment?" I dared.

"Letitia stayed with us quite some time ago. She thought she wanted to stay, then she met her dragon and eloped with him. She said he was from a town called Havenwood Falls, where she was originally from as well, and she returned with him to become the family matriarch there. We never heard from her again," said a woman appearing to be in her early sixties, with Easter egg purple hair piled up on top of her head and a glint of hurt in her eyes.

"Granted, we were not living so close at the time. We didn't know how to get ahold of her," Grace supplied with a sad shrug.

"She was a lot of fun back in those days," a different woman commented with a big smile—I thought her name was Gladys.

"That sounds like Aunt Letti," I said with a smile before I realized I had.

"So are you all hunters?" I asked, looking around the room at each of them.

"Most of us are," Rachel chimed in, "but we have human members who have married into the family and offspring that are either human or half hunter."

"Really? Some of you are half hunter?" I was surprised to hear that and realized I rambled. "That's pretty cool, I mean it makes sense, but we don't have any. Offspring from a hunter and a human where I am from produce either a full human or a full hunter—one or the other. And in my family the girls are mostly hunters and the males are human."

"Except for your brother," Charlie put in.

I nodded. "Except for Brice. So how can you be half hunter?"

"A half-hunter half-human mix basically dilutes the full hunter experience. They can sense the same things we do, but only at half the strength," the older boy on the floor explained without taking his eyes off his screen.

That made sense.

Rachel turned to me, a suspicious expression on her face. "So you can't tell which of us are hunters or not?"

"I should be able to, right?" I asked, uncertain.

"Oh yes, definitely," Sunny blurted, nodding her head. She was like a cute little ray of sunshine on caffeine. Brice would be so annoyed.

"I'm learning, just a little slowly, I guess. Back home, my mom doesn't inform us of everything until our eighteenth birthday—though I see that needs to change." Now that I said it out loud and looked at those around me, it seemed a silly thing. I should have known more about being a hunter. I should've known what to expect when I began to experience symptoms.

"No. Way," Luke and Jeremiah said at the same time, in stereo, really making a girl feel confident.

"You mean, they don't let you be a hunter, or fulfill your responsibilities as one until you are eighteen?" Charlie asked, her jaw practically hitting the seat of the couch.

I had already learned my lesson. I wasn't about to tell them that not only did we live near witches and agree to suppress our hunting nature to be a part of their community, but that I also had a witch boyfriend. Wow, the shit would really hit the fan in this room if I did.

"I guess when you put it that way, it doesn't sound quite right," I admitted, trying to think of something to change the subject.

"What do you do where you live then?" Sunny chirped.

"I guess the same as any teenager. I have a job, I work at a coffee shop. I hang out with friends, I go to school—hey, speaking of, why aren't any of you at school?"

"Oh, we homeschool," Charlie answered.

"We move around a lot," the older boy, still intent on playing his game, answered flatly.

"Do you have a boyfriend?" Sunny asked with stars in her eyes. She couldn't be more than twelve maybe.

I hesitated, feeling the blush suddenly rush up my neck.

"Ooh you do! I knew it!" Sunny practically bounced in her seat. "Is he a human?"

"Uh . . . no, not exactly," I hedged. I took a step backward, looking to Grace. Dizziness suddenly swam in my head. I reached up to try to keep my head from rolling to the floor.

"Hey, are you okay?" someone asked.

"I'm not sure. I feel funny. Grace? Did you give me something else?"

"No, dear." She sounded worried.

As quickly as it hit me, it was gone. Widening my eyes, I looked around the room. Nothing had changed, but I felt something in my head I couldn't explain. Rolling my shoulders and neck, I shook it off. "I'm not sure what that was, but it's gone now."

"Is he a dragon, like the one your aunt married?" Sunny asked.

"What?"

"Your boyfriend, is he a dragon or another shifter? Or maybe a vampire?" My potential answer had her on the edge of her seat, more intriguing than the games being played on the screens in front of her.

"He's a witch, isn't he, dear?" Grace totally outed me, and I didn't know why.

"WHAT?" roared too many people's voices to differentiate. I had to hold my hands over my ears.

"What kind of Blackstone are you?" Rachel's vehemence shot at me.

"The kind who lives above the archaic prejudices you seem to be stuck on," I shot back. I would not be put down because of who I chose to hang out with. I edged myself back toward the wall slowly, not wanting to appear like I was backing down, but needing to move around. A window came into my view. I needed to see where I was.

"Careful, you're in our house, Macy," Charlie warned.

"Yes, and not by my choice. Is kidnapping something you're all okay with? Because I'm pretty sure the law wherever we are is not."

I heard a couple stifled laughs.

"We're outside the law, Macy. You should be thankful that we found you in time and brought you here where you can learn your hunter side safely before somebody got hurt," Rachel informed me.

"What are you talking about, before somebody got hurt? In time for what?" I asked, totally confused and yet feeling the stirrings of something inside me that felt dangerous and desperate to be freed.

"If your hunter surfaces and you don't know how to control it, something terrible could happen. If you got out of control, you might even hurt an innocent passerby without meaning to. An unchecked hunter is dangerous, Macy," Charlie added, sliding a look over to Rachel, then back to me.

I thought of Gallad. I shouldn't have at that moment, but I couldn't help it. I was out of control, and I did hurt an innocent.

"She's right," Rachel jumped in. "And just think if you did happen to come across a witch while your hunter tendencies flared to life and you weren't ready for it or the witch. You could get hurt. Witches are powerful and dangerous, especially when threatened by a rabid hunter intent on killing them."

My heart started jumping in my chest. I would never hurt someone intentionally, let alone kill them just because they were a witch. Glancing out the window, I noticed a street, then a park down below, maybe three stories. Not too far, but I'd still probably break something, or a lot of things, if I jumped. But maybe I could figure out how to get outside.

The room closed in around me, and shortness of breath assaulted my lungs. I could feel my eyes frantically searching for anything to use to my advantage.

"Macy, are you all right, dear?" Grace asked from somewhere near me, her voice echoing like in a cave. "You don't look so well."

"I think you should lie down," Charlie suggested.

"Is she going to throw up?" Sunny's little voice asked with slight disgust.

"Eww, no, get her out of here," one of the boys yelled.

"Yes! Air, I need air," I begged. Holding one hand against the wall so I didn't fall over and the other against my chest, I grabbed at my neck collar, hoping to alleviate the tightness in my chest. "Grace, where is my phone?"

"I . . . I'm sorry dear, I don't know. Dante took it into his office."

With my limited ability to discern the situation around me, I noticed Charlie glare at Grace for even telling me that much.

"Come with us." Rachel stood up and gripped my upper arm with her warm hand. "Charlie, help me. We'll take her out to the courtyard for some air."

"Thank you, thank you," I panted, practically clawing at Rachel's shirt. Charlie came up and took my other arm, supporting it as they led me out of the room. Instead of going back to my room the way we had come, we descended a stairwell I hadn't seen on my way in. Two flights down, the landing opened up into an unassuming entry complete with a solid wood door—the gateway to fresh air.

Rachel punched a code into a keypad to the left of the door so fast there was no way I could have seen which numbers she put in. Charlie reached forward and opened the door as soon as the green light next to the keypad indicated it was unlocked.

"This is a short visit outside. We can stay out longer tomorrow, but why don't you catch your breath and sit for a minute. I'm sure it's a lot to take in." Charlie almost sounded caring or even understanding. But I didn't trust her tone, no matter what her words suggested.

"Thank you." I gulped the fresh air as we stepped out into it. Closing my eyes, I took a moment to slow my heart and my breathing. Rachel tugged my arm.

"There are benches in the courtyard out here." She pointed to a little area to our right. It was small, but still managed to include a lovely garden area and a pleasant seating area with a table, chairs, and an umbrella. Along the bottom of the high fence were several benches put end to end to create a long one. Hearing the soothing sounds of water, I jerked my head back to see a fountain at the end of the area.

"It's really nice," I whispered genuinely.

"It is. We enjoy it most evenings. We even have a fire pit at the other end," Charlie said as she pointed to it.

Rachel and Charlie seemed to relax a bit as they led me to the seating area. They kept me close, and their eyes never left me.

"Doing better?"

I nodded slowly. "I think so. My breathing has slowed down a bit, but I'm still dizzy."

As I answered, the fence opened from the outside, and a mail carrier walked in with a package. The girls said hello, and Rachel jumped up to receive the package. While she signed the slip, the postman handed Charlie the rest of the mail. Out of the corner of my eye, I spied that the gate had not latched. Now was my chance.

I stood up and swooned dramatically, my hand draped across my forehead. I gasped as I started to fall forward. All eyes turned to me in surprised confusion, but mail dropped all over the ground as they leaned forward to assist me. In the moment of their shock, I bolted for the gate, flinging it wide and slamming it behind me. I didn't know where I was or where I was going. I simply ran.

Yes! It worked. I knew I should have gotten an A in drama last year.

After a half hour of running faster than I knew I could, making sure no one was following me, I stopped in a busy area by the side of a street. I had nothing. No phone. No backpack. No ID. No money. Nothing. This sucked. But I was free.

Spying myself in a nearby shop window, I was shocked to see my eyes were bright and fevered. Perhaps I wasn't faking what I was feeling as much as I thought I was. My breathing was still shallow, but more normal than it had been. Shaking off the edges of dizziness that legitimately plagued me, I looked for anything that could help me.

"Excuse me," I asked a nice-looking elderly woman, though cautiously, since the last elderly woman burned me.

"Yes, can I help you?"

"Could you tell me what the name of this town is?"

She looked at me funny, probably wondering if I was a runaway. "You are in the outskirts of Durango. Do you need help?"

So not that far from where I was before then. Good. My parents knew I was in Durango. Maybe they were looking for me!

"You don't look so good, child. Can I call someone for you?"

Could she? "Do you have a phone I could use?"

The woman retrieved her phone from her bag and handed it to me after unlocking the screen. I opened the phone app and started to dial then hesitated. "I . . . I can't remember the number . . ." I frowned and shut my eyes tight. "Why can't I remember the number?" I whispered harshly to myself.

"Take your time, dear, it will come to you."

Inhaling a deep breath, I simply dialed something without thinking about it. Thankfully it rang, though I had no idea who I just called.

"Hello?" a man's voice answered.

"Daddy?"

"Macy? Baby, are you okay? Where are you?" His voice was rushed and panicked.

"I'm okay, I think. I'm outside Durango, but not sure where. Dante Blackstone and crew took me to their home. Can you come get me? Tell Mom. She'll know what to do about them."

"Where have you been? No, we can talk later. I want to get on the road. Macy, find somewhere safe. I'm on my way. It will be late when I get there. Do you see a restaurant or something near you we can make a meeting place?"

Looking around, I saw several shops, a bakery, a restaurant, and a few taverns. "There's a small park across from a restaurant called Jimmy's that's open late. I'll find a place to wait there, then meet you at the restaurant."

"Be safe, baby. We'll be there as soon as we can."

"Maybe Uncle Tranner could get you here faster," I suggested of Aunt Letti's dragon husband.

"I'll see what I can do."

"I love you, Daddy."

"I love you, too."

I handed the woman back her phone and thanked her before I ran across the street to the small park to look for a place to hide. The sun was already going down, and hopefully I could use that to my advantage.

CHAPTER 12

*H*ours later, the full darkness of night had fallen upon the outskirts of Durango. I was still sitting in a tree I found that allowed me to pull my legs up and hide. I felt like such an imposter cowering in a tree. It wasn't in my nature. I was supposed to be a hunter. And I was getting hungry. I hadn't seen or felt any sign of hunters nearby, or anyone at all, for that matter, in quite some time. I ventured down to see if I could find food without having to resort to stealing or begging.

Hopping down from my safe haven above ground, I scouted my route through the forest at the edge of the park. I could make out the street I had been on earlier. People still milled about, but most were patrons of the taverns, which could be their own kind of trouble. The chilled air had a bite this late at night as the weather descended into fall. I jumped around to get my blood flowing. Sneaking through the copse of trees like a spy, I watched where I stepped and stuck to the shadows. Once a break in the dense canopy opened, I looked up to find the moon at its peak fullness. Unexpectedly, my arms tingled, and the sensation traveled up to my shoulders.

Uh-oh. I hadn't felt that since I was in Havenwood Falls, but I knew it meant I was near a witch. I thought I was alone out here. More carefully, I headed toward the people. If I was near more people, perhaps I had a better chance of blending in. Almost to the edge of the park, I felt the warmth at the back of my neck too late before I saw the shadow of someone up ahead. A hunter. Not knowing who it was, I kept my guard up. Of course they had felt me, because everyone was better at being a hunter than I was. Did I take my chance with them? Or head the opposite way and try to avoid the witch? I recalled what Charlie and Rachel had said earlier: when the hunter surfaced for the first real time on their own, they could lose control.

Taking my chance with the witch, I turned and hightailed it as fast as I could go away from the hunter. I had no idea where the park ended or if it even did. Outlines of mountains in the distance were visible in the moonlight. Distinguishing if there was a river or thicker, denser trees was almost impossible from my location. Someone watched me; I felt eyes all around me, closing in on me. Similar to the feelings I experienced earlier at the house, the nausea and dizziness came over me, but so much more intense.

My vision blurred. I heard things on either side of me that didn't sound natural, but I couldn't be sure. My stomach rolled. A new sensation, one of epically toxic proportions, punched me in the gut. *Black magic.* I doubled over, thankful I had eaten nothing to bring back up. The buzzing in my ears brought with it a fogginess that swarmed my eyesight. I was about to faint as the toxic sludge forced its way through my veins.

I stumbled forward, urging myself to move.

I ran blind, as fast as I could. I ran faster than I should have been able to. My ears burned with sensitivity at every sound of the forest all at once. And my sight, instead of going completely black, sharpened and went into some kind of night-vision mode. If I didn't know better, I'd say I was turning into a shifter like Ruby or our friend Willa Kasun's family back home at Havenwood Falls, but I did know better. My hunter side was surfacing in full force, and I had no idea what to do about it. One thing I did know for certain—I needed to stay away from the witch.

Feeling a sharp poke in my butt, I swatted my hand and came back with a small needle-like thing with a fluffy top. Someone hit me with a tranq dart! I kept running.

The next thing I knew, the ground jumped up to smack me in the face. Voices screamed my name, and then I blacked out.

"Macy! Macy! Oh my god, you have to wake up!" A panicked female voice shouted at me as hands shook my body.

Groaning, I tried to open my eyes, but they felt so heavy. "What happened?"

"You killed a witch," her voice said with a bit of pride.

That did it. I jolted my head up and forced my eyes to open. Looking around, I was on the ground not anywhere near where I thought I had been. In front of me was a body of a young man about my age, his neck at an odd angle. I leaned over and threw up, or at least tried to, but I had nothing. Tears ran down my cheeks. I studied my hands. They felt foreign to me, capable of such a deed. I sobbed uncontrollably —the vision of the corpse forever burned in my mind.

"Macy, get a grip!" Rachel crouched down next to me. When she had my attention she continued. "We had just found you when you ran from us, then you went crazy like an uncontrollable animal, screaming. We followed you, then we sensed the witch. But we got here just after you took him down. You were so fast! Then you passed out," she explained.

"I . . . I don't understand . . . how could this have happened? What do I do?" Panic tore through my chest. My dad was on his way. Oh no! My dad was on his way, he couldn't see this, couldn't know his baby girl killed someone. The other Blackstones had been right. My hunter was out of control. Something was wrong with me.

"Macy. It's time to come back to the house with us before the authorities find the mess you made." Dante spoke unfeelingly from the side as he looked on. "Let us train you, prepare you for next time."

I was numb. "I deserve to be taken to the authorities. Let them come to me," I said quietly.

"Don't be silly. It's just a witch," Charlie said from somewhere beyond me.

"Shut up, Charlie," another voice hissed. Nala. I recognized her voice, but hadn't seen her since I had been with the Blackstones. "Give her a minute. She'll come around."

"Macy, we cannot allow you to be caught by the authorities. It puts us all in jeopardy. We will correct the problem. You will be trained and won't lose control again. This one here," Dante pointed to the body, "was dabbling in black magic. Did you notice a toxic feeling as you got closer to him?"

I nodded. I would never forget that sensation. I remembered feeling it back in Havenwood Falls before I left, too. The Luna Coven would want to know about that for sure. The thoughts of home pierced my heart. I couldn't go back, even if I wanted to or if I tried to. They wouldn't let me now that I had done the unthinkable. Gallad would never look at me again. I had nothing and nowhere to go.

Dante held his hand down to me expectantly. "Will you come back with us?"

Hesitating, I found no other option. I nodded.

Dante whispered behind me to someone, telling them to clean up the mess. We headed back to the Blackstone compound.

"If you let us, we could be your new family."

Numbly I followed along with Nala and Rachel on either side of me to what would be my new home.

BACK AT THE COMPLEX, I received my own room. It turned out I had been using Sunny's room before, as she was the only one willing to give it up for me. This one was plainer than plain, with nothing more than a twin bed complete with a beige comforter, a plain white dresser, and a small wood desk. No window. It didn't matter. I didn't deserve to be comforted by the light of day. I showered, then curled up on the bed and cried myself to sleep.

I woke to a hissing sound. With no idea or concern for how long I had slept, I covered my head with my pillow, went back to sleep, and dreamed of Gallad.

In the dream, he called to me, his voice a soothing balm. He spoke to me as if I could respond to him, but I remembered what I had done and tried to shut him out. Gallad was relentless and persistent—telling me how much he missed me, and I needed to come home. He talked about random things, as though filling the time. He told me my dad was searching for me. Could I tell him where I was? But I couldn't speak. Hearing his voice was more than I deserved. It wasn't real anyway, but I could allow myself this indulgence for a moment.

"Tell me about school, Gallad." I finally tried to talk to him. Since it wasn't real, what could it hurt?

"What do you want to know, Macy?"

"Everything. I miss you so much, it hurts." I cried some more but kept it to myself.

He proceeded to tell me exactly what I had asked for—everything. Gallad went on to share with me about all his classes, his teachers, the other students at Havenwood Falls High School. It was our senior year, and I was missing it. Gallad was on the football team, but his heart wasn't in it this year, he said. People kept asking about me and when I was coming home. *Home.* I didn't have the heart to tell him it could no longer be my home.

"Macy, I have to go now. The sun is coming up. I'll try to contact you again. The full moon assisted me this time, but I don't know when the next time will be," he explained, though I thought I had a pretty good imagination for concocting such a story for him. "Don't forget me, Macy. I will always love you."

His voice faded out of my mind. "Oh Gallad, you wouldn't if you knew what I had done," I whispered to myself as I woke up fully to the sound of knocking at my door.

"Time to get up, Macy. Training starts in one hour!" Sunny chirped too cheerfully for any time of day, let alone after just waking up.

That's exactly how my days began for the next week. Training. Breakfast. Schooling. Training. Free time. Dinner. More Training. Bed. I was exhausted.

Training consisted of working out intensely with weights, aerobics, and yoga. I was also educated about how the hunter gene worked, the different sensations I felt, what they meant, how to control them so they didn't overpower me, and how to use them to my advantage. I worked harder and studied more than I ever did at home. Every evening ended with yoga training. I didn't remember doing it before now, but my body already knew the moves, and I loved it. Something tugged at the back of my mind, perhaps a memory, but I couldn't place it. After an intense day of training, we gathered around the fire pit out in the courtyard and roasted marshmallows.

Every day that went by, the ache in my chest for somewhere called home grew less and less. I knew I had a mom and a dad and even siblings, but some days it took longer to pull up my memories of them or the sounds of their voices in my head. The layout of the town I came from, and even its name, sometimes eluded me like a lost memory trying to resurface, poking its head out occasionally for air to survive one more day, then be forced back under the water of forgetfulness.

"Macy," Dante called me into his office one day. "You have been excelling at your training. How are you fitting in here?" he asked.

"I'm beginning to feel like this is home. I know Charlie doesn't really like me, but I'm used to her and can hold my own."

"Do you miss home? I was thinking it was time to return this to you." He pulled out a desk drawer and handed me a cell phone. I rubbed my forehead where a slight headache had been forming.

"This is mine?"

He looked at me strangely. "Do you not remember?"

"It feels familiar in my hand, and I'm having flashes of memories, but they're not strong." I rubbed my head again. "I can't remember some things. I feel like the memory is there, but it takes me longer to grasp than it should."

"Why don't you go through your phone and see if it brings back any memories. Maybe call your mom or dad. I was thinking it was time to arrange a meeting with them so you could visit. Would you like that?" He watched me carefully for my answer. But I wasn't sure how I felt. Part of me wanted to jump up and down and say yes! But part of me wanted to hide from it, from the thing I had done, the shame I still felt.

"I think so. Could I take some time with this to see what I remember?" I asked, feeling odd I was even asking at all. My chest felt tight with emotion, but I wasn't sure why.

"Of course. You know where I am if you need to talk." Dante stood up from his seat and waited while I exited his office. I paused outside his door, hearing him talk. I thought at first he was still talking to me, but I paused before responding. My sensitive hunter hearing came in handy sometimes.

"She's starting to forget. We can't let her forget how to get home. If you see it get worse, let me know. We'll have to move up our timeline." He hung up what must have been the office phone.

I quickly dashed down the hall, using my new stealthy skills they had instilled in me. What had he been talking about—a timeline? What for? Lost in thought, I almost ran straight into Nala at the end of the hall.

"Oh! Sorry, Nala, I was lost in thought," I rambled when I was thrown off.

She cocked her head, watching me. "You all right, Macy? You seem off."

Off? Yeah I'd say so. "I just have a headache. Do you have anything I could take for it?"

"Grace does. I would find her. Maybe get some sleep too."

"I haven't been sleeping well. I know I'm having dreams but I either can't remember them in the morning or they're of people and places I can't put my finger on."

"Get some sleep then."

Yeah, thanks, Captain Obvious.

"Thanks," I said politely as she moved passed me. I turned around and went to find Grace. Her room was on the second level, and I made my way straight there. I didn't have to wait long after knocking on the door.

"Macy, lovely to see you, dear." Grace moved aside and welcomed me into a room twice the size as mine.

"Thank you, Grace. I have the mother of all headaches beginning and Nala said you might have something to take the pain away?" I asked, pinching the bridge of my nose after she offered me a seat.

"I do indeed. Just a moment." Grace walked into a bathroom and came back holding a bottle.

"You have a bathroom in your room?" I was so jealous.

She laughed. "I do." Grace handed me a couple of the small pills and a glass of water. I swallowed them quickly.

"Thank you." I downed the rest of the water. "Grace, I never asked you . . . well, maybe I shouldn't. I mean, I'm wondering how you are related here, especially to Dante. You're a hunter, right?"

She nodded. "Yes, dear. Well, technically, I'm half hunter, half human. As such, we age more closely to a human but get a few extra years in there. I am Dante's granddaughter at eighty-five years old."

"Well you look pretty good for eighty-five. I had you around mid-seventies." I smiled at her. "I hope I didn't make you uncomfortable asking."

"Of course not, child." She patted my arm and sat down in the chair next to me. "I see you have your phone back."

Looking to the device in my hand, I held it out. "I do, though I don't remember it very well. I get glimpses of memories and just when I think I have a solid grasp on them, they fade from my mind. It's infuriating. Dante thought maybe if I looked through it, I would remember more. He said maybe I should try and call my parents . . . Their names are slipping past me, though. Ugh. Why can't I remember? I feel like I should remember more." I flung my head down on my arm on the table in a most dramatic fashion.

"The important things will come to you, dear. Though I remember when Letitia started forgetting things, she found writing them down was helpful for a time."

"But why am I forgetting? I can't even remember that!"

"Seems there was something she said about wards and protecting the town from outsiders, though she didn't tell me too much. Said I talked too much, but I don't know what she could ever mean." Winking at me, she raised her own glass of water and took a sip.

I opened my phone like I knew how to do it and powered it on.

Immediately it started buzzing, and text message after text message popped up, accompanied with voicemail notifications. The very sight was overwhelming. Dozens of messages of concern, love, and worry were left by names that rang a bell but not clearly enough to give me a visual impression. Obviously, the ones titled "Daddy" and "Mom" had to be my parents. But the ones from Gallad stirred something strong in my chest—a mix of emotions from pain and guilt to joy and excitement. It was fuzzy, but something about his name brought an image of green eyes that pierced my soul. Thinking of pictures, I opened the photo app and scrolled through the images of me with other people, some who looked like me. Visions of places and names of people and voices flooded through my head, but almost as quickly, they funneled back out.

"AH! I almost had the memories strong enough to latch on to them!" I mimicked grasping at them with my hand into a fist. My head started hurting again. It was more than a headache this time. It was almost like a pinprick behind my eyes.

"Maybe I should just call somebody and see what they say, do you think?" I asked Grace as she watched me carefully with concern and almost sadness. "Don't be sad, Grace. Maybe I'm not meant to remember." I sighed. But deep down I really wanted to remember. The pictures of those people looked like they had a ton of fun. A girl with strawberry-blond hair posed with me in some kind of rock T-shirts, making funny faces. There were more of me and a very handsome guy with the same green eyes I had just envisioned. Others might have been family, but I couldn't place them.

"Yes, Macy, I think that might be a good idea," Grace confirmed.

"Grace? What's the date?" I asked, not even sure why I did.

"It's September twentieth. Oh, and it's also the new moon tonight, ushering in the autumn equinox tomorrow."

"Well, aren't you full of information?" I laughed, but something about what she said nagged at the back of my mind. Probably something else I forgot about. I went to the voicemail app on my phone and listened to the first message.

"Macy, it's Mom. I don't know where you are, and I hope you're okay. I believe in you, so I know you're okay, you have to be. There's a lot we need to talk about. I'm sorry I didn't prepare you the way I should have. None of this would have happened otherwise. Please come home, baby. We miss you. Gallad's going out of his mind, showing up every day, asking about you. Today is September seventeenth. I just want to remind you in case you are already starting to forget things . . . after twenty-eight days, September twenty-first, you will forget all about Havenwood Falls. It's a safety precaution, but right now I'm ready to overthrow the Luna Coven to keep you remembering. I wish I could. You will forget about your family. Me, I'm Lilith, and I'm your mother, Daddy is Reggie, your brothers are Brock and Brice, and your best friend is Ruby Jean. And you'll forget how to get home. Please know, we will never stop searching for you and believing you will find your way home. I love you."

That was the end of the call. Slowly, tears found their way from my eyes down my cheeks and onto my lap. Her voice brought up an image of her face. She had outlined everything I basically needed to know right now.

"I have to call her back!" I fumbled with the buttons on the phone as my eyes kept blurring from the tears. Grace handed me a tissue without saying anything, and for that, I was appreciative.

Finding her number, I hit the button, but nothing happened. I wiped my eyes, sure I had hit the wrong one, and tried again. Nothing.

"What is wrong with this thing? It's not working!" I looked up at Grace. She, too, had a tear in the corner of her eyes.

"I'm so sorry, Macy, I don't know."

Desperately, I tried again and again, until right after my last attempt when there was a sizzling sound, the phone vibrated, and then the screen went black.

"What just happened? No, no, no, where did everything go?" Frantically I tried to power it on, but nothing happened. It was dead. "It fried." I stared numbly at the phone.

"This won't do." Grace tsked to herself. "I must tell Dante."

"You do that," I mumbled. "I'm going to my room."

"Macy?"

"Huh?"

"Write down all you can remember immediately. Describe pictures, sounds, names, everything. Before you lose it all again, but this time for good," she warned softly.

I nodded and left her room. I had lost my family once again.

CHAPTER 13

*A*fter a somewhat awkward dinner with everyone at the long table in the dining room, I heard some of the girls talk about starting up the fire pit, and some were going to play cards. I couldn't shake what I had heard on my voicemail, and I was doing everything I could to hold onto the images and descriptions I had seen, to the point of ignoring the others.

"Macy? Macy!" I heard my name shouted repetitively.

"Oh, what?" I looked around for the source of the shouting.

"I said—after several tries, I might add—are you all right?" Rachel asked.

I had a sudden case of déjà vu from not too long ago, when I couldn't come to terms with my hunter side and tried to run away. A few memories from even before that, before I came to Durango, started to resurface, but they felt fuzzy.

"Sorry, I have a headache." To prove my point, I rubbed at my forehead.

Nala sat quietly off to the side like she often did and watched me closely.

"We forgot to grab the new bag of marshmallows, Rachel," Sunny whined as she looked through the basket of supplies they brought out.

I stood up. "I'll get them. I want to get more aspirin from Grace."

"Thanks, Macy!" Sunny beamed and did a little skip around the pit and into the courtyard.

Before I got to the door, I felt eyes on me. Looking around then finally up, I spotted Dante watching me from his office window on the third floor of the five-story building. Unabashedly, his eyes followed me until I couldn't see him any longer, but when I turned back around before entering, I caught Nala giving him a curt nod. What that could be about?

After I retrieved the entire bottle from Grace, I made my way up to my room to grab a sweatshirt. Nights were too cold for long sleeves alone. I made the decision to try to enjoy tonight with the girls. The boys had opted to go to a movie in town with some of the adults that had come back from a recent hunting trip out of state. So there were more people milling about inside than normal. Practicing my stealth mode, I crept lightly down to the end of the hall where Dante's office was. Whispers had reached my sensitive ears, and I was simply a snooping teenager. Something was going on, I could feel it. I just didn't know what.

Getting as close as I possibly dared, I held completely still and even slowed my breathing.

"Dante, she's not doing well. Something needs to happen to force the issue, otherwise she'll forget everything for good." Nala. I thought I left her outside. Guess that was what the nod was for.

"Tonight is the new moon and the cusp of the equinox. Perhaps the energies could intercede and assist us." Dante's voice seemed thoughtful.

"What do you mean?" asked one of the adults I hadn't talked to much—I thought his name was Bob. He was Charlie's father.

"She hasn't gone out on a hunt yet since she's been trained. Let's set one up for tomorrow, a celebration to thrive in the autumn equinox and the turning of the seasons. Witches will be out in force. We'll call it an initiation," Dante expounded with satisfaction.

"I'm unsure where you're going with this, sir?" Nala asked. "I don't think she's ready for a hunt yet."

I fist pumped for Nala. I didn't think she would be the one to stand up for me.

"You misunderstand, Nala. The hunt won't be real," he began.

Wait, what?

"It will be the catalyst that sends her over the edge. Because you're right, she's not ready. I need her to try to find her way home. I need her to lead me to Havenwood Falls—there will be a treasure trove of not only witches but the rest of *my* family." He slammed his hand on something, creating a loud noise. "My sister Marie took them from me, hid them from me, and now I have the one chance we've been searching for to lead us straight to them."

Insert maniacal laugh accompanied with creepy music here, please. What the hell? They've been using me?

"They will either join me in my quest to bring all witches to justice to pay for their crimes, or they too will pay for theirs."

"Oh no," I whispered. I quickly made it back to my room. My heart beat heavily in my chest, my breathing quickened. Not knowing what to do, I paced in the tiny space of my room.

"I can't believe they used me! I can't believe I didn't see it!" I whispered, in case someone walked past and heard me.

"Sit on the bed, Macy. Calm down," I told myself. I breathed slowly —in through my nose, out through my mouth.

"Macy? Macy?" another voice called to me. I went to the door, but no one was there. I didn't have a window, and even then, I was three floors up.

"Macy, can you hear me?" The voice was urgent and the most intoxicating masculine voice I had heard. It called to something deep inside me. Looking around, I couldn't find the source.

"Hello?" I whispered back.

"Thank the goddess you can hear me!"

"Where are you? I can't find you."

His enticing chuckle rang through my head all the way down to my toes, affecting me in ways I hadn't remembered feeling before. But maybe I had.

"I'm in your head, so to speak."

Cocking my head, I was totally confused. I moved my jaw around, popping my ears, and shook my head.

"Still there?"

"Yes. Unless you learned how to block my spell, you can't get rid of me." His voice sounded sad now.

"Who are you?"

Silence flooded my head, the strangest feeling.

"You don't remember me?"

"I'm not sure. Your voice is familiar. Do you have green eyes? I'm envisioning green eyes."

"I do. It's okay, there's not time to explain it all right now. The wards are really strong. I should know, my family helped create them."

"Are you from Havenwood Falls? That name keeps coming up."

"I am. Just know that I'm a friend—well, more than a friend—and I care about you."

"Okay . . . Are you the guy that was in pictures with me on my phone?"

"I hope so, otherwise we have another set of issues." He chuckled again. I really liked the sound of it. "Yes, I am. My name is Gallad Augustine. I'm your boyfriend. At least, I was when you left us."

By the hurt I could hear in his voice, he must have really cared about me, maybe even . . .

"Do you love me, Gallad?"

"With all my heart and soul," he breathed out with so much emotion, it gripped my heart and squeezed tight.

"Things are going down where I am, and I'm not sure what to do about it. You contacted me for a reason. So what can you tell me?"

He told me all about Havenwood Falls and where I lived and my family and friends as quickly as he could. He had given me enough information that lined up with some of the pictures I had seen for me to trust the stranger in my head.

His relief was almost palpable through our mind connection, though I had no idea how he was doing it. He had said "spell." Did that mean . . .

"Gallad, are you a witch? Is that how you're speaking to me?"

He hesitated. "Yes. It's a spell I have been trying to get through to you with, but I think the added energies from the equinox helped strengthen it."

"Then you and your family are in trouble." I proceeded to tell him what I had heard from Dante and the others. Gallad took everything in stride and didn't freak out like I had. I told him everything I could remember, even the part where I took the life of another witch . . . that I would never forget.

"Gallad, I have to get out of here. I know they are setting me up, but I can't go through with an actual witch hunt to play along and not give away that I know their plans."

"Here's the plan. It will work with your current situation." He told me what he, along with my parents and something he called the Luna Coven had come up with.

"Founders Day . . . is that the day with all the outdoor games, like the three-legged race and tug-o-war?"

He paused. "Are you remembering it?"

"I'm not sure, but maybe. I also saw some pics in my phone that had you, me, the girl you called Ruby—please don't tell her I didn't remember her—and some other kids in front of a gazebo with a banner that said 'Founders Day' on it."

"That's the one. So it begins in the morning, then after dark is when the covens gather at the falls to strengthen the wards around the town. You should be able to feel the power, or energy, from quite a distance. Let energy and the images I'm putting in your head guide you."

I laughed quietly. "Sorry. It makes me sound like I'm a computer you just plugged your thumb drive into."

He laughed, too. Talking to him had completely calmed me down, centered me, and brought me a peace I forgot I had until now, when I was with him. He reminded me I didn't need to be a hunter who lived like a traveling nomad and killed witches. There was another way.

"Macy, be careful. It could be dangerous, and it will be dark."

"I will. And Gallad?"

"Hmm?"

"I can't wait to remember you."

~

LATER IN THE EVENING, the adults had finally come outside to join us by the fire. It was late, and night had fallen like a black blanket. Several of us huddled under blankets to keep our backsides warm away from the fire.

"I have an announcement," Dante said from where he leaned against the brick façade of the building, not sitting by the fire with the rest of us. "Tomorrow ushers in the autumn equinox and the turning of the seasons. We are going to celebrate together by going on a hunt."

A few cheers erupted and shouts of "yeah," "about time," and "we'll get those witches" fed the darkness. Dante turned an eye on Charlie and some of the boys who had joined us as well.

"Voices lowered please, Charlie and Luke. We have neighbors with ears," Dante growled. A few others, whom I had only recently met as they had been out of town hunting, joined the group for the announcement.

"Am I to go on this hunt, too? Do you think I'm ready?" I asked, nervously. No lie there.

Dante searched my face in the dark, then nodded. "I believe you are. It is time."

I nodded back, unsure what my response should be. It would raise suspicion if I showed any excitement.

~

THE NEXT DAY passed way too slowly with the anticipation of what was to come that evening. Like all other days, we trained and even did some schoolwork, then we waited it out by playing a huge round of video game racing. I had never played so many video games before—at least I didn't think I had—but it helped time go by. Evening finally arrived and with it, a full case of butterflies for what I was about to do.

On our way out, all the hunters and I said goodbye to the humans that stayed behind. As I passed Grace, I felt a mix of sadness to leave her, but also hurt at her betrayal to me the entire time. I don't know why I hoped for an ally in her, maybe because she knew Letitia Blackstone, who I think was my aunt, from what Grace had said. She reached out and grabbed my elbow.

"Be careful out there, Macy. Always follow your heart. It will lead you home," she said quietly.

I cocked my head and frowned at her. Did she know my plan? Did she mean to come back here if I got separated from the group? Simply patting my arm, she whispered, "You'd better get going."

"Right. Goodbye, Grace," I replied and turned to follow the others outside into the night.

I was so glad I geared up with warm clothes. The other girls had pitched in to give me clothes to wear, and Dante surprisingly had one of the adults shop for me. I layered on as many clothes as I could. I had no idea how long I might be out in the cold night.

"Come on, Macy, keep up!" Rachel hollered at me from the front of the group. "It's your first hunt. Are you excited?" she said with exaggeration to pump me up, failing miserably.

"Um, I'm not sure about excited. Nervous, definitely nervous." Better to be honest, I thought.

After a lengthy time of walking, we entered a denser part of the forest nearby. Dante had instructed that there was a coven of witches he had heard about across the river, in the next community north of ours. My nerves rose with each step I took. My heart fluttered in my chest. I felt like everyone was watching me, waiting to see if I would go through with it. Of course, they weren't all watching me; it was my own paranoia about who knew the insiders' secret. Finally approaching the river, I could hear it rushing by from quite a distance away. We slowed, looking for the bridge to lead us across to the coven. The tingling in my arms started growing stronger and stronger the closer we came. They weren't lying. There really was at least one witch across the river. And judging by how strong the tingling was, I'd say there were definitely more. Due to the training I had received, the sensations in my arms no longer bothered me. No longer were they uncontrollable.

Thinking about it, I either had to go through with the hunt and watch these people who called themselves my family wipe out an entire coven of witches in one night, or I had to create a diversion and leave immediately. I knew what I had to do. I'd always known deep down— there was never really a choice.

"I . . . I can't do this," I announced. Everyone turned to face me. I was met with expressions of satisfaction from those who hadn't expected me to go through with the hunt and anger and hurt from those who had.

"You what?" Rachel shouted with anger.

"I'm sorry. I'm not meant to stay with you."

With that, I took off at a dead sprint. I knew they would follow me. However, I didn't expect the loud expletives shot my way. But I kept on running. I could feel the hunter in me emerging as I ran faster and faster. Unfortunately, many of them were gaining on me, running almost as fast.

I followed the river for a time, knowing it led north. I could hardly remember anything, but I knew I had to go north until I started climbing the mountain. The darkness surrounded me, but my night vision kicked in to guide my path. The terrain was rough but I maneuvered it better and more smoothly than I had anticipated. I knew the others would have the same advantages—I only hoped my determination would outweigh theirs. After a few minutes, I didn't hear as many of them as I had before. Perhaps some of them turned back.

The path grew steeper and steeper the more the ground climbed toward the mountains. I saw a reflection of the light from the sliver of moon where the river curved around a boulder and headed toward the east, away from me. The sight brought back a flash of an image I had seen recently, but couldn't remember why. The night approached midnight of the autumn equinox, and I felt something stir inside me. I didn't know what, but it felt peaceful, so I let it lead me. Almost instantly, the pictures I had seen before, when that guy had spoken into my head, came rushing back into memory—what was his name? He said he cared about me. Gallad! That was his name. He told me to follow the pull—the pull to what? I couldn't remember, but I trusted him, I knew that much. Other landmark sights started popping into my head, so I turned toward them or swerved around them, but follow them I did.

I didn't know how many hours had gone by, or where I was, but I was exhausted. I didn't hear anyone behind me, but that didn't mean they weren't there. Dante had said they wanted to follow me somewhere —I couldn't remember where, but it was where I was trying to go, where what's-his-name was leading me . . . Ugh! Gallad! Why couldn't I keep him in my head?

The farther I went, the more defeated I felt. I couldn't remember most of the time where I was headed. I only followed a gut feeling and the pull of my heart toward somewhere north. I hoped something or someone waited for me when I got there, because I was the one being hunted now. The Blackstones were the epitome of stealth, but I still felt that faint warmth behind my neck, indicating a hunter was near.

Unable to take one more step, I stopped to rest for a minute. My breathing was labored, and my heart was about to explode through my rib cage. If I stopped for long, though, I wouldn't want to keep going. I never thought I might die from exhaustion until now, but it was highly plausible. Voices sounded in the distance, though I couldn't discern how far away or who they were.

"Macy? Can you hear me?" the voice in my head spoke to me again.

"Where are you?" I panted, catching my breath.

"You're close, Macy. I can feel the connection between us stronger than before."

"I don't remember where I'm going. I keep trying to remember you, but right now you're my conscience. I know I trust you, but the memory of you keeps slipping through my fingers!" Tears fell down my face, air stuck in my throat as I hiccuped, and I crouched down, lowering my head in defeat.

"I believe in you, Macy. You have always been strong. Know that I love you, trust that. We're waiting for you."

"Where do I go?"

"Look up into the sky. Can you see the light coming off the horizon in the east, where the sun begins to rise?"

I looked but didn't quite see it from where I was near the ground. I stood to see better. The sky was beginning to lighten to my right, though just barely. He must be higher up than I was still.

"Yeah, I think so."

"Head that way. Your real family is waiting for you."

My real family. I wish I could remember them.

I turned around to smack right into Sunny. Cute little Sunny snuck up on me, and I had no idea how.

"Sunny! You frightened me. You shouldn't be out here so late. Are you alone?" I cautiously looked around her, but didn't see anyone. I couldn't believe they would let her out this far on her own. Yes, we might have been hunters, but we were trained specifically for witches—there were still a lot of other dangers in the forest, especially at night.

"I followed you." She shrugged like it was no big deal. "I'm better at following than the others."

"What happens now?" I tried to determine what her purpose was in following me.

"I . . . I just wanted you to know I heard the older girls talking about how they set you up when you first came to live with us," she started, uncharacteristically shy.

I didn't have time for this. She was stalling so the others could catch up, I was sure. She piqued my curiosity, though. "What do you mean?"

"You didn't kill that witch."

"Yes, I did. I woke up and found him."

"You don't remember. They shot you with a tranq dart and staged the entire thing so you would come and stay with us. Charlie is the one who killed him." Sunny looked mad and yet also unsure. I almost felt bad for her. If I could take her with me I would, but then I'd be a kidnapper like they had been to me. When she was older, she could choose.

"Sunny, when you're older, if you ever want to join my family, I will find you." I watched her reaction, but her expression changed. She looked much older than she had seconds ago.

"Thanks, Macy, but why would I want to do that? I'm having fun for now." She turned to leave.

"That's it? You're leaving? You're not telling the others where I am?"

"Nope. You should be able to leave if you want. But I thought you should know the truth. Bye, Macy." Taking off at a run, she didn't even look back.

"Goodbye, Sunny."

That was my cue to head toward the rising sun.

CHAPTER 14

*V*oices assaulted me from overhead. I was so focused on putting one step in front of the other, I almost didn't realize someone called my name. I was beyond exhausted, but had to keep going.

"Macy! Macy!" A woman yelled to me.

I looked up, almost blinded by the sun, but there on a large rock jutting out over my head was a woman. She was older than me, but looked like me with blond hair and the same sharp blue eyes. Running down to meet me was a man who was old enough to be my father with kind eyes the same shape as mine. He, too, called me by name. Could they be . . . could they be my parents?

"Macy! You're really here!"

"Are you all right? Get her some water, somebody!"

"Where are the others? Are they following you?"

All the voices blurred together. I stopped and sagged to the ground, falling to my knees. I had nothing left. The woman ran down to join the man.

"Did I find you? Are you my parents?" I mumbled, my mouth dry from dehydration and exertion.

"She doesn't remember, Reggie. She's still beyond the wards." The woman sank in front of me, pulling me to her chest. Sobs wracked her body. "I'm your mother, Macy. And I'm so sorry. I knew you could do it."

The man next to her embraced us both, also crying. "I'm your daddy, Macy. We were so worried, missed you so much, didn't know how to find you . . ." All his words came out in a rushed jumble.

I didn't know how much time went by. They slowly administered water to me in small doses so I wouldn't be sick and gave me food, too. Slowly I recovered enough to stand up. They helped me and wouldn't let go of me until I was strong enough on my own.

"Let's go home," the woman who called herself my mom said.

"Yes, let's." A man's voice preceded him as he stepped out from behind a large rock formation. I froze. Dante.

"Oh no," I whispered. "They did follow me. I'm sorry."

"It's part of the plan," my daddy whispered into my ear. "Just wait."

"Dante, I see you haven't changed," my mother addressed him, standing tall, every bit the hunter as the rest of those coming up behind Dante. She appeared strong and fierce. I'm sure I knew she could be, but I still couldn't remember.

"Indeed, I have not." He inclined his head like he was being properly introduced. "It's nice to see you, Lilith. I enjoyed getting to know your protégé." He waited for a response, but when she gave him none, he continued, "You look very much like my sister Marie when she was young. Where is she? I should like to say hello." He sneered in the subtlest way, his intention quite clear in his eyes.

"She died back in 2000. I'm sorry to be the one to inform you," Lilith replied flatly. "But somehow I think the sadness of it will be lost on you."

Something flashed across his eyes, disappointment to not get to face her or that he didn't get to kill her? Or perhaps genuine sadness for the loss of his sister?

"Odd she would die still quite young. Might you know why, matriarch of your family?" He taunted her.

"I do, in fact. Because we have chosen not to hunt witches and kill them for sport, our life spans are shortened without the excess energy in our bodies."

I didn't know that.

"Very good. Did you also know that I have many male hunters in my family? I heard you might have one in yours? I'm sure you know how you get one of those, too?" Dante smirked, not waiting for her answer. My mom stood proud, unmovable. The only thing she gave away was the slightest twitch in the corner of her eye, but unless you looked, no one would have seen it. I would have to ask her about that. Based on her expression, my mom had no intention of replying to his comment.

"Now, if you'll continue, we would love to be introduced to your quaint little town. Havenwood Falls is it?"

"Dante, you will never see Havenwood Falls. We won't let you." My dad stepped up to the plate. Though he was a human, he apparently was a badass one.

Dante laughed in his face, but my dad stood strong. "Oh and I suppose you are going to stop me. You and what army?"

He gestured to the hunters standing behind him, lined up and awaiting instructions. Many of them glared at me, but some refused to look at me, including Nala. I thought I could find a friend in her, but I guess not. The only one remotely curious or pleased to see me was little Sunny. I couldn't even believe she was still with them. I gave her a curious look, but she held her finger up in front of her mouth, telling me to keep our secret.

"This army," Lilith said without removing her gaze from Dante. As she said it, other hunters from our family stepped from behind trees and rocks where they had apparently been hiding and waiting, wielding a variety of menacing weapons. Then the biggest surprise was the witches, who stepped out in droves. My arms tingled so badly, I had to grip them to keep them from shaking. How were my mom and the other hunters so still, so unaffected by their presence?

Dante grimaced and released a growl unlike any I had a heard a man make. The other hunters shifted on their feet, prepared for a fight. Instead they got a huge surprise when the witches started a spell in unison. Holding out their hands, they blew a red sparkly dust. With the aid of the wind, the dust carried straight into the faces of all the hunters standing with Dante. I scrambled back closer to my parents, not wanting to get hit with whatever that dust was.

Dante and the others batted at their faces as they turned and headed the opposite direction, down the mountain. My mouth gaped in awe.

"What just happened? They were going to fight, and now they're leaving?" I asked, baffled.

"The witches came up with the plan with the help of your boyfriend, Gallad. It is a forgetting spell that will misdirect them temporarily and cause them to forget what they were searching for. However, it's only temporary. Once the wards are reinforced, they will be redirected anytime they come close again," she explained, helping me up to my feet again.

"Thank you," I said, but then turned to face everyone there. "Thank you, all of you." I sobbed out a hiccup and wiped the tears from my eyes again. It was all over. I was safe.

"Can we go home now? I'd like to try to remember it," I asked sheepishly.

"You'll remember everything just fine, sweetheart," my dad said, reaching for my hand, and I let him take it.

"How can you be so sure?"

"Because the wards are created to protect the town, but once you're back in it, and with the help of the Luna Coven, you should regain all your memories," Mom supplied.

"It could be a slow adjustment, though, so don't get discouraged if it's not instantaneous," my dad added.

"Then let's go home."

"Not until I get to see her," a young male shouted from behind a crowd of witches as he pushed through. Tall, athletic, with floppy brown hair and sharp green eyes I would remember even in my darkest moments—he had to be Gallad. I couldn't remember my connection with him, other than I had one. My arms tingled even more as he came closer. I had to fist my hands at my sides to keep them from shaking again. *Breathe in through my nose and out through my mouth.* I didn't want to hurt him.

"You helped me get home," I stated, not taking my eyes off him as he strode slowly forward. I felt stalked as he did so. The witch pursued the hunter.

"I did. I couldn't go on without you," he whispered roughly, but my ears heard it clear as a bell.

"I felt you here," I placed my hand on my heart, then on my head, "and here, guiding me."

"I knew you could make it." He believed in me from the start.

"Can you forgive me for leaving?" I felt small like a child, but I had to ask, had to know.

"Always," came his reply.

I couldn't stand the distance anymore. I ran toward him and threw myself at him, knocking him onto the ground. Hearing the gasps and shouts from those around us, I pulled back but Gallad wouldn't let go. He gripped me tight and held me to him.

"Stop, Macy. Don't hurt him," hunters shouted at me.

"Get out of the way, boy," the witches yelled.

I looked up in utter shock. "You all thought I was attacking him? Give me a little credit. I learned to control my hunting side—kind of," I said, looking down at my shaking hands, but Gallad covered them in his at his chest. Looking into those eyes, I asked him, "Did you think I was attacking you?"

"Of course not. I might not mind if you did, though." He winked at me. I couldn't believe he actually said it. Though he was still a stranger to me, I had to remember that we had a history and maybe talked like that all the time. I giggled, embarrassed others were watching.

"I didn't kill that witch. They set me up," I confessed to him, since I had told him the entire story.

"I didn't believe it for one minute," he stated, and I saw the truth in his eyes. "My Macy could never do that, even in the worst situation."

My Macy, he had said. It warmed my heart, and I melted into him.

"I can't wait to remember you."

"So you've said." Gallad laughed, then kissed me on the lips in front of everyone, including my parents.

My dad cleared his throat. "Okay, show's over. Let's get her home."

EPILOGUE

$\mathcal{T}$he week after I returned home was supposed to be for me to rest and regain my memories. Some came back all in a rush when I crossed the border of Havenwood Falls, but others still came slowly or as events and people were brought up. It was maddening how slow it was at times. My parents had given me the week to get ready to start school once October came. Plus, I had agreed my mom could put me through orientation, a sort of Hunters 101, on my eighteenth birthday, October thirteenth.

Gallad and Ruby had come to the house every day, or I met them in town at Broastful Brew or Coffee Haven, depending on the day. I was told I could start up work again part-time at Broastful Brew this fall when I felt ready.

Gallad had shared how he told my parents everything I had told him once he was able to communicate with me. My mom interjected that Aunt Letti had shared with them details of the hunters and her stay with them. My grandmother had been instrumental in retrieving Letitia with her husband a long time ago, and had been introduced to Dante then. My mom had met him later, but I still didn't know the story there yet. She hadn't realized they had been so close to our home. Mom blamed herself, saying she should have known. But after my ordeal, she set a watch schedule for the hunters to be on the lookout for Dante's possible return and even posted someone in the town of Durango on and off to keep tabs on them.

My mom had apologized profusely that she had not prepared me sooner. She thought she still had time, so she let me keep pushing her away. She was upset she hadn't forced the issue, though that rarely worked out well. My mom was not one to apologize, so it was a big deal.

I told Mom and Dad outside of Brice's hearing that Dante did in fact have other male hunters, and I wanted to know why we didn't have any other than Brice. He was going to ask, and I didn't want him to be blindsided like I had been.

"I will tell you, Macy, I promise, but it's not for right now. I will explain it to you and Brice as he gets a little older," was all Mom had to say, though her eyes glossed over with the pain of a time she would have rather forgotten. I guess I had to take it one step at a time with my mom.

The first full day I was awake—I slept the first real day—members from the Court of the Sun and the Moon accompanied by the Luna Coven came to see me. They wanted a full report, which I gave, leaving nothing out. They had asked if I was prepared to receive my Havenwood Falls tattoo, to choose to be a full-fledged citizen of the town, even though I wasn't quite eighteen as my family's custom dictated. It was close enough. They explained how it would work.

Some might say I was trading my freedom to be less than I was created to be and marked by a town in secrecy. All I had to do was envision Gallad's bright green eyes and I knew my future was with him and this town. It was the easiest choice I'd ever made, and in that peace, I felt the freedom I desired.

The day before I would go back to school, Gallad surprised me. I was helping out at the vineyard, soaking in the afternoon sun, and relishing the smells of grapes and smoke from the fire pit as we burned debris in preparation for winter. The aspens had turned colors, and fall was in full swing. It was everything that I loved about living in the mountains. He brought our friends with him to the vineyard and had pre-arranged with my parents a bonfire party to celebrate my official return. As the evening fell and the stars became visible, I realized I could never see the stars and night sky anywhere in the world like I could in my own backyard. It was amazing.

"Macy?" Gallad called from the other side of the fire towering above my head.

"Where are you?" I hollered back, giggling.

"On the other side!"

When I rounded the large fire, passing various friends, I found Gallad standing in a circle of things I loved. Grapes, a stack of books, small glow-in-the-dark stars, one of my pink coffee travel mugs with steam escaping the lid, a bowl of kettle corn, a pile of scattered notes of welcome from my friends, a bottle of my favorite wine from my family's vineyard, and a few things I had given Gallad over the last couple years. I was so stunned, I didn't know what to do.

"What . . . ?" I barely got out, as suddenly my throat was choked up.

"Macy, these are all the things you love . . ."

"With you at the center of them," Ruby shouted playfully behind me, and everyone giggled or agreed around us.

"Yes, I'm hoping I continue to be at the center of them." He gave Ruby a wink, then turned back to me. "Macy, will you go to homecoming with me? The theme this year is *Written in the Stars,* and I want you to know I would travel through time and space to get to you, always."

"Yes! Of course I will go with you!"

I ran to him inside the circle and kissed him full on the mouth. It was going to be an epic time to remember.

I KNEW Dante and the other hunters would eventually seek out a way to discover Havenwood Falls again, but for now I, and the town, were safe. We'd be ready for them. The Blackstone family of Havenwood Falls would protect their own; we had the weapons to prove it. When I saw the witches and hunters carrying the weapons together in the forest I was amazed, but finding out they were our own creation that we made secretly to protect the town, I was even more in awe at my family.

I once thought I had been denied my heritage by suppressing the darker side of it. Truthfully, once I received my new permanent tattoo, the one I chose to be marked with, I realized I was free to be me without the extra fight. I still had all my other hunter tendencies—I would never be denied those—but I could control them and use them to protect the town I loved. I had truly been reawakened, and I never wanted to forget again.

～

WE HOPE you enjoyed this story in the Havenwood Falls High series of novellas featuring a variety of supernatural creatures. The series is a collaborative effort by multiple authors. Each book is generally a stand-alone, so you can read them in any order, although some authors will be writing sequels to their own stories. Please be aware when you choose your next read.

OTHER BOOKS in the Young Adult Havenwood Falls High series:
Written in the Stars by Kallie Ross
The Fall by Kristen Yard
Somewhere Within by Amy Hale

COMING SOON ARE books from Michele G. Miller, Cameo Renae, Randi Cooley Wilson, E.J. Fechenda, and more.

IMMERSE yourself in the world of Havenwood Falls and stay up to date on news and announcements at www.HavenwoodFalls.com. Join our reader group, Havenwood Falls Book Club, on Facebook at https://www.facebook.com/groups/HavenwoodFallsBookClub/

ABOUT THE AUTHOR

Morgan Wylie is an award-winning and *USA Today* Bestselling author with several genres published from YA fantasy to adult paranormal romance, as well as other stories in between! Morgan published her first novel, *Silent Orchids,* one year after moving across the country with her family on a journey of new discovery. After an amazing three years in Nashville, Tennessee, and the release of two more books, Morgan and her family found their way back to the Northwest, where they now reside. Still working every day with great optimism, Morgan continues to embrace all things: "Mama," wife, teacher, and mediator to the many voices and muses constantly chattering in her head, where it gets pretty loud!

You can find her and news on her books at the following:
MorganWylie.net
Morgan Wylie Books on Facebook
@MWylieBooks on Twitter and Instagram

ACKNOWLEDGMENTS

First, I'd like to thank Kristie Cook for her amazing imagination and her generous heart to include others in her vision of Havenwood Falls. It's an honor to work with her and the other wonderful authors that are quickly filling up Havenwood Falls! I've loved working with her; her attention to detail, organization, and patience has strengthened me as a writer.

Next, a big thank you to my family—my husband and my daughter —as they were so supportive and patient with me while working on this project. I wouldn't be who I am today without them. And to my first readers on this project: my mom and my #LoveWriteCreate crew, Gaby Robbins and Kallie Ross. Thank you.

And last, but definitely not least, I'd like to thank YOU, the reader. Thank you for your support and for hanging out in Havenwood Falls with me!

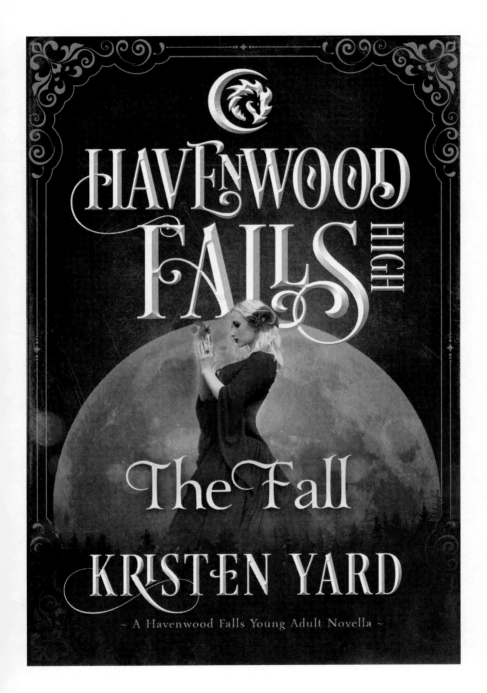

HAVENWOOD FALLS HIGH

The Fall

KRISTEN YARD

~ A Havenwood Falls Young Adult Novella ~

AN EXCERPT

The Fall (A Havenwood Falls High Novella) by Kristen Yard

Seventeen-year-old Serena Alverson is drawn to water. She spends much of her time by the falls, sketching the beauty of life's sustenance. An introverted "late bloomer," she has no interest in a social life aside from her two best friends, Logan and Nikki. She's never had a serious boyfriend and has rarely left the safety of Havenwood Falls.

Serena has big dreams for her future, things she wants for herself after high school—to travel and study the great artists of the world while developing her own craft. To break free from the sleepy little town she outgrew by age eight. But her carefully laid plans fall asunder when she receives a gift from her aunt, a mysterious necklace with the power to sear her skin. With each burn, she questions her sanity. It doesn't help that an ominous figure starts shadowing her steps.

When Mother Nature finally comes knocking, she hands Serena not only her womanhood, but also a wicked lifetime curse with the potential to destroy everything and everyone she loves. For water also has a dark side. Water is birth, water is life . . . water is death.

THE FALL

AN EXCERPT

*L*ight glimmers through the ceiling of a cavern. Moonlight morphs the water into a sea of diamonds, bobbing gently against rock walls. Water roars in the distance. I sit up, assessing the situation.

Where am I?

How did I wind up in a cave, when I swear I just laid my head down for a quick couch nap? Glancing down at my bare feet, I note the dirt on them. *Where are my shoes?*

I steady myself and then rise to my feet, looking for an exit, but there isn't one. My heart ricochets off my rib cage as I run my hands along the wall, edging my toes over the tiny strip of stone separating me from the water.

"Help!" I call, sifting through memories of the day, trying to piece together what could have led to this.

School, then a Coffee Haven stop with my best friend, Nikki Morris, and her new boyfriend, Max Cooper, then home, and couch.

So how am I here? And what is this place?

My mind flashes to the lagoon behind the tiny distributary waterfall that runs from Havenwood Falls into my own backyard, but the lagoon looks nothing like this. There is definitely an exit to that cavern.

My hands go clammy. Max was the one who grabbed our coffees from the barista and brought them to the table. Logan Andrews, my and Nikki's other best friend, is convinced that Max brought not only designer clothes, but also designer drugs with him when he moved here from New York City.

He drugged us. That's it. Oh my God. Nikki.

Whatever fear I have for my own well-being takes a back seat to the throat-tightening terror of picturing my bestie tied up in a trunk —or worse.

"NIKKI!" My voice breaks into a sob. Then I clamp my hands over my mouth, realizing that Max might still be in the vicinity. *What if I got away and am now luring him back to finish me off? No. I have to find a way out and call for help.*

Losing my footing, I slide down onto my knees, my arms flailing out to catch me before I fall into the lagoon.

I fight to catch my breath and then notice a sound that picks up over the surrounding cacophony of rushing water.

Whispers. Layers of them, building upon one another.

I freeze, trying to focus in, past the rushing falls, so that I can understand what they are saying. All the while, my mind begs me to run, but I cannot move.

The whispers finally come together into one voice.

"Serenaaaaaa."

It comes directly from the water in front of me. With a gulp, I take a breath and then lean forward, until I am directly over the brackish pool.

The inky clouds clear. An emerald light shines from below the surface, revealing a woman in the depths. Her blond hair cascades around her in waves, concealing her face.

I lean in closer, and the current finally moves enough of her flaxen strands that I can make out her features. A porcelain face with a pointy chin, long eyelashes, a slightly turned-up nose, and full, pink lips. The birthmark on her left cheek sends my heart stuttering, but when her eyes snap open, revealing piercing blue irises, I scream.

Because the girl in the water is me.

Her eyes glow. She shoots up, water droplets glittering around her.

She smirks and then pulls me in, as I scream and kick, trying to break free.

∾

"SERENA? SERENA!" Aunt Odette yells, as I attempt punching my way to freedom. "Hey! Million Dollar Baby! It's just me, your adorable aunt, trying to wake you up to give you cake and presents. Can you please refrain from killing me?"

I blink a couple of times. The warm glow of the fireplace and the log walls of my family's cabin releases the knot in my stomach.

"You feeling okay, honey?" Aunt Odette's face eclipses my view of the room. Her sky-blue eyes narrow in concern, and she places a hand on my forehead.

"Yeah . . . just a wicked nightmare."

"You want to talk about it?" she asks, rubbing my shoulder.

I shudder. "No, I'm good."

Slowly, I sit up and stretch, shaking the dream off. "So, what's this you said about cake? And did you make it yourself?" I ask, eyeing her, because I love my aunt, but she cannot cook to save her life.

She grins. "Yes, I did. But no worries. I've been practicing! Oh, Serena." She sighs in disapproval.

"What?" I yawn.

"Your feet are filthy. Next time, can you please clean them off before you put them on the furniture?"

The knot returns to my stomach, and I lean over to examine them. My eyes frantically search through the pile of shoes by the door, and I try to remember what I had worn to school. Sandals would explain dirt, but it's too cool for sandals. *It was a dream. How would this even be possible?*

"Okay, okay, I'm sorry for channeling Grandma. That even weirded *me* out," she says, misunderstanding my reaction.

I let out a nervous laugh, and she pulls me to my feet, smoothing my hair.

"And about that cake, oh, ye of little faith. You never know, it could actually be the best of your life." She winks and leads me into the chilly October night.

We walk through our yard, nestled beside Mount Alexa and surrounded by the woods on all sides. Our roaring mini waterfall is a curtain to the lagoon I explored as a little girl, sitting behind our cabin. The thought of it brings me back to the cavern in my nightmare, speeding up my heart, as my mind continues to try making sense of what just happened.

The memory of glowing eyes in the water quickens my pace toward our family's business, the Fallview Grill & Tavern, which is on our property, but higher up the mountain.

"Why are we going here instead of just eating in the house?" I ask.

"Man, are you writing a novel or something? Why all the questions? Maybe I just didn't want to burn the house down. You know, since you think I suck at all things culinary."

"But your heart is in the right place," I offer.

She snorts and then gestures toward the entrance of our restaurant. "Hey, can you open the door? I messed my back up earlier."

"How?" I ask in concern, holding the door open for her to pass.

"SURPRISE!" a group of people shout. I fall back against the door, laughing as my aunt winks.

"Gotcha!" she singsongs, leading me over to the small gathering of our family and friends.

The rustic lodge vibe of the tavern is at odds with the very feminine lavender and silver streamers, balloons, and number-18 decorations strewn about.

Nikki and Logan come up to me first. In the time since we left school this afternoon, Nikki's long wavy brown hair has been hacked into a shoulder-length bob. I gasp as I take it in, flashing Logan a confused look. He barely nods in what I take as quiet agreement that he's as shocked as I am by Nikki's new do.

"Oh!"

"Ya like?" she asks.

I gape at Nikki, because her hair has been one of her most prized physical traits as far back as I can remember.

Her face falls. "You don't like. Clearly."

"*I* don't like," my little sister Laurel pipes up.

Nikki narrows her eyes. "Nobody asked you, Felicia."

"Laurel!" Lena, my other little sister and Laurel's twin, scolds her, as I glare at Laurel. She shrugs. Her white-blond hair shines under the lights as she plops down on the couch and starts texting someone. My phone beeps. I pull it out of my pocket and then turn toward Laurel after reading the text.

"You couldn't just say 'happy birthday' instead of texting it?"

She shrugs again, and Lena comes up and gives me a quick hug.

"Happy birthday, sis."

"Thanks, Bug,"

When I glance up, my best friend still looks aggravated.

"Nikki, I think your hair is adorable. You just caught everyone by surprise," I protest, wrapping my arms around her.

"Happy birthday, babe," she says, kissing my cheek.

Honestly, Nikki's new look does frame her pixie-like features, high cheekbones, and doe eyes to perfection. It's just that she has been undergoing some pretty weird and major personality changes over the past few months, which have left Logan and me worrying. The brooding dark-haired guy in expensive clothing trailing her is one of Logan's biggest concerns when it comes to Nikki's strange, new behavior.

"Hey, Max," I say, still uneasy from his appearance in my dream. Misplaced or not.

"Happy natal day," Max says.

I blink and then smile, but Logan rolls his eyes.

"Hey," I say to Logan when he wraps his broad arms around me, pulling me in for one of his famous, all-encompassing hugs. His familiar woodsy scent nestles around me.

"Happy birthday, Rena. Sorry. My, uh, dad couldn't make it," he says to Aunt Odette, who waves it off.

"One Andrews is plenty, and you're my favorite of the lot," she teases, knowing as well as I do how much it hurts Logan that his dad is such a workaholic. Mr. Andrews owns a contracting firm that builds cabins for anyone, from the professional mountain man to the tourist who just wants to build a summer home. He has allowed work to become his new wife in the wake of Logan's mom's death a few years back.

"Thanks for coming," I say, extricating myself from the awkwardly long hug.

Logan grins and slowly releases his hold.

PURCHASE *The Fall* at your favorite book retailer.